ANIMUS

Based on True Events

by

Brian W. Smith

This is a work of fiction, and names, characters, places, and incidents are strictly the product of the author's imagination. Any resemblance to actual persons, living or dead, events, or locales is entirely coincidental.

Copyright © 2021 Brian W. Smith

All rights reserved. No part of this publication may be reproduced, stored in, or introduced into a retrieval system, or transmitted, in any form, or by any means (electronic, mechanical, photocopying, recording, or otherwise), without the prior written permission of both the copyright owner and the above publisher of this book.

an·i·mus

noun
 1. Strong dislike or enmity; hostility attitude.

1
August 26, 2005 / McKinney, TX.
5:07 a.m.

"**M**ama," whispered young Robert Sumina. The nappy-head, five-year-old boy with ears that appeared too small for his head and eyes that could serve as the headlights on a Volkswagen, fidgeted in the mouth of the hallway. Those large eyes toggled from his mother to his foul-mouth father squatting in front of the floor model television contorting the rabbit ear antenna.

"Mama," Robert said again, his voice a little louder to get his breastfeeding mother's attention.

"What baby?" Crystal Sumina lazily replied; her focus remaining on six-month-old, Enis Jr., who'd locked on to her nipple like a leech on an open wound.

ANIMUS

"Mama," Robert called a third time with a hint of urgency in his voice.

"Crystal, answer that damn boy!" Big Enis barked and smacked the side of the television. "I'm so sick of this piece of shit, tv!"

"Robby, can't you see I'm…"

The rest of Crystal's sentence faded when she saw the horrified look on her son's face. She reflexively looked at her husband and then back at Robert. In a tone that hovered just above a whisper she asked, "Robby, what did you do?"

Robert's lips didn't move, but his tear-filled eyes screamed. The same way dogs respond to dog whistles that only they can hear, mother's respond to non-verbal cues from their kids that only they can hear.

Crystal cradled Enis Jr. and stood up. She glanced over at Big Enis who was now smacking the television harder. The television protested the assault by offering an ashier screen. Big Enis fired off a few more expletives.

Crystal scanned her son for blood, but there was none. Her anxiety lowered from a 10 to a 7—this wasn't life or death. She looked for signs of different colors on his fingers, but there were none. Her anxiety dropped from 7 to 5—this wasn't something that required primer and paint. Just as she was about to instruct Robert to go fix whatever mess he'd created, she noticed Robert's jeans were wet around the ankles and his feet glistened. Crystal's anxiety spiked to 10 again.

"Robby, what happened?" Crystal whispered.

Robert backed away slowly—a non-verbal cue for his mother to follow him.

With EJ nestled under her shirt enjoying his noon feeding, she tip-toed out of the living room and followed Robert down the hallway. The twenty-six-year-old mother of two was unsure of what level of mischief awaited her at the end of the hallway, but her maternal instincts told her it was bad. In this case, her instincts were wrong. The level of mischief that awaited her could only be described as *terrible*.

ANIMUS

When they were a few feet away from the bathroom a stench that rivaled the smell emanating from the sewerage plant across the street from their house attacked her nostrils.

"Robby, what did you do?"

Robert didn't respond but his eyes said: *I fucked up.*

Young Robert managed to unfurl an entire roll of toilet tissue and shoved it in the toilet. After ensuring the roll was lodged firmly in the commode's throat, he flushed a few times and watched in amazement as the toilet coughed and gurgled. When the brown water rose to the rim and settled, he flushed again. That's when it happened. The toilet vomited. Feces tainted water spilled onto the bathroom floor and created a pool big enough for the boy to splash in.

Unsure of what to do, Robert did the only thing he could think of—he ran and told his mother.

Crystal couldn't hide her fear. She understood that five-year-old boys were prone to such bad decisions. After all, they were alleged to be made of frogs and snails and puppy dogs' tails. Clogging the toilet seemed like the kind of act that the good Lord hardwired them to do. But she also knew the depths of her husband's fiery temper. He would not be so understanding once he spotted this mess.

"Dammit, Robby," Crystal muttered. She used her free hand to pull the boy in the bathroom, locked the door, and surveyed the scene. "We've gotta clean this up before your daddy sees it."

Those tears that were forming seconds earlier spilled from Robert's eyes. He didn't mean to cause a mess. It was just an experiment gone awry. From the moment he became potty trained he marveled at the way the mouth at the bottom of the toilet bowl swallowed its food. He was curious to know how much it could eat before it became sick—now he knew. One roll of toilet tissue was more than the porcelain god's stomach could handle.

"I'm sorry, Mama."

ANIMUS

"It's too late to be sorry. We've gotta clean up this mess. Get all the towels out of the dirty clothes hamper and spread them over the floor so we can soak up this water."

Robert yanked opened the small door in the corner and pulled out a hamper large enough for him to climb in. He grabbed four large dirty towels and spread them on the wet floor.

"Good, good. Now, I want you to get the plunger from behind the toilet and stick it in the toilet. Do it slowly because the water is gonna gush out."

The trembling child waded through the water on the floor; looking back at his mother with every nervous step he took. With wide eyes and a furrowed brow, his mother motioned frantically for him to move faster. Robert adhered and gripped the plunger by its wooden handle. He'd often wield it like a sword when fighting imaginary creatures, but never used it for its intended purpose.

Robert shot one last glance at his mother before lowering the plunger into the toilet. More murky water spilled—and so did tears from the chocolate child's eyes.

"Now shove it a few times and then pull it out slowly."

Robert did as he was told, but his efforts were futile. The toilet belched but the clog remained—and so did the anxiety that waffled between he and his mother.

"Robby, I want you to hold your brother."

Crystal handed EJ to Robert, making sure the baby's head rested perfectly in the crook of the five-year-old's arm. EJ squirmed and whined, but Robert was too busy watching the stubborn toilet to be concerned with the protest of a greedy infant.

"Hold him tight, Robby. I'm gon' try to unclog this toilet. I don't want you to ever do this again. You hear me?"

"Un-huh."

"What?"

"Yes, ma'am."

ANIMUS

Crystal was in the middle of her third thrust when the doorknob rattled. Seconds later, the door shook from the weight of Enis' large hand pounding on it.

"What's goin' on in there? Why is water coming from under the door?" Enis banged on the door again. "Open this damn door!"

Crystal froze. She considered leaving the door locked while she worked but knew it would only make Enis angrier. And for what? The odds were great that the toilet would remain clogged anyway. It was better to let the big bad wolf in so he could get his belligerence over with. She backed away from the toilet, took EJ from Robert's trembling arms, and nodded at the door.

"Unlock the door for your daddy."

Robert's eyes spoke up again: *Woman, are you crazy?*

"Go ahead and open it, baby."

Robert hesitantly pressed the button on the knob. There was a click. Enis barged in like a raging bull. Flames raged in his beady eyes as he surveyed the catastrophe.

"Get out!" Enis shouted.

Robert didn't have to be told twice. When Crystal failed to move as swiftly as his command warranted, the bully shoved her out of the bathroom causing his wife to stumble and nearly drop the baby. Enis was too blinded by rage to notice anything other than the overflowing toilet.

Enis traipsed through the water and grabbed the handle of the plunger like it owed him money.

"Robby, you'd better hope I can unclog this toilet because if I can't, I'm gon' beat yo' ass until my arms get tired!"

That was the type of foreshadowing young Robert could have done without. His body quaked when he heard the threat. His father often hurled threats around the way rappers toss around the word "bitch", but this one seemed more venomous than the previous ones he'd issued that week.

Crystal's eyes darted from the hallway that led to the front door then to Robert and back to the hallway. The front

ANIMUS

door of the shotgun-styled house was roughly twenty steps from where she stood. Even with the screaming baby in tow and Robert glued to her hip, she could probably make it out of the front door before Enis unclogged the toilet or admitted defeat. But what good would running do? Enis would surely catch up to her, grab her long ponytail, and drag her back caveman-style in the house.

Rather than use energy she'd probably need to recover from the sure-to-come beating, she found the nearest corner in the rat-infested house and retreated to it.

"Come here!" Enis ordered.

"He didn't mean to do it, Enis. If you hold the baby, I'll get in there and clean it up."

"Shut up woman before I wipe this nasty ass floor with your face." Enis pointed at Robert and growled, "Come here you little bastard."

Robert wedged himself between his mother and the wall and clung to her like a joey on the back of a mama Koala.

"Enis, you ain't gotta do this. He's five-years-old. He don't know no better."

"He gon' know better after this ass whoopin'."

Enis traveled the distance between them with three long steps and yanked Robert up by his collar. The boy's grip of his mother's shirt was so tight that he nearly pulled it over her head as he rose to the eye level of the six-foot monster whom he called, *dad*.

"When I finish with you, you gon' think twice about clogging the toilet. I'm gon' beat the living—"

Enis' sentence was cut off like fingers in a garbage disposal. His eyes widened and his face contorted. He could hear a chomping sound. It was the sound he heard when he watched his grandfather shove a gutting knife into the belly of a deer. He didn't look down until he felt a warm and wet sensation in his mid-section.

Enis released his grip and clutched his stomach, which coughed up blood the way the toilet had coughed up shit.

ANIMUS

"You lil bastard. You stabbed me."

Robert looked at the second mess of the day he'd caused. The blood was dark red and created a red bullseye in the middle of Enis' white t-shirt. Enis grimaced. Robert smiled...and stabbed him again.

"I hate you!" Robert shouted and sprang up in bed panting as if he'd just run a marathon. Beads of sweat dotted his forehead. He examined his hands and mumbled, "I...I hate you."

Melody turned on the nightstand lamp and found her husband of ten years panting and sweating profusely.

"Baby, are you okay?"

Robert nodded.

"Another nightmare?"

Robert nodded again and rested his head on the headboard. He used his clammy hands to wipe his brow and the sweat trickling down the side of his face.

Melody got out of bed and went into the bathroom. She returned seconds later holding a large towel. Robert sat as still as a newborn baby while she wiped his forehead, face, and chest.

"You wanna talk about it?"

"I was a little boy. I clogged the toilet. He got mad and was about to beat me. My mother tried to protect me, but she really couldn't because she was holding EJ. When he grabbed me, I stabbed him in his stomach. I don't even know where I got the knife from. It just appeared in my hand and I stabbed him. I woke up right when I was about to stab him again."

"Baby, you've been having these dreams for as long as we've been together. It's not normal to always dream about killing someone...especially, your parent. I really think you should talk to Dr. Miles again."

"I think you worry too much," Robert said and took the towel from Melody. He wiped his back. "I'm forty years old and I've made it this far without relying on a shrink; I think

ANIMUS

I'll be okay. I told you once before, I'm not going back to that man's office." He kissed her gently. "Now go back to sleep."

2

August 26, 2005 / New Orleans, LA.
9:33 p.m.

Enis Sumina moved around the front of his Honda Accord as fast as his sixty-five-year-old joints would allow and opened the passenger door. A grin wide enough to show his remaining twenty-eight teeth appeared as he marveled at legs that looked as if they were sculpted by Michelangelo.

The African goddess emerged from the car rocking synthetic hair—which was too blonde to ever be convincing on a black woman of her complexion—that danced in the stiff breeze. The painted-on dress she wore hugged a butt that women paid to have and men paid to kiss. She was the kind of thirty-something every "old man in the club" hopes to nab

ANIMUS

when he puts on outdated clothes, takes a bath in Lagerfeld cologne, grabs his #1 Granddad gold chain, and shamelessly heads to a nightclub filled with people half his age.

"Damn this wind is strong!" Enis shouted over the howling wind.

He slammed the car door, grabbed her hand, and they scurried toward the stairs that led to his second-floor apartment. Had he tempered his desire to devour the fish who'd nibbled on the one-hundred-dollar bill he used as bait at the bar, he might have noticed the black SUV that followed him home—stalking him like a predator waiting to pounce.

The temperamental weather could be attributed to the line of thunderstorms preceding a Category 5 hurricane that was headed their way. Hurricane Katrina had just tap-danced on Cuba and, according to meteorologist, was in the Gulf of Mexico breakdancing its way toward Louisiana.

Winded by the time they made it to the top of the staircase, Enis closed his eyes, gripped the railing, and took in a few deep breaths via his nose.

"You okay, baby?" asked the woman. "Maybe this isn't a good idea. You seem like you're out of breath already. I don't know if you're ready for this young ass."

"Girl, I was born ready."

Once the hallway stopped spinning, Enis staggered over to the apartment that he believed was his and leaned against the door. He fumbled the keys but managed to grab them before they fell.

Lord, it's been years since I had a shot at a piece of ass like this. I know I ain't been a model citizen, but I'ma need you to take care of a nigga tonight. If you do, I swear, I'm gon' go to church every Sunday. Wait...no I'm not. That was a lie Lord, my bad. But I ain't lying about this...if you just let me get hard long enough to get about five strokes without vomiting all over this chick, I'm gon' go to church at least twice a year. He squinted. *Where did all these keys come from?*

Enis only had four keys on his ring, but he'd downed four Rusty Nails—his favorite scotch drink—in a two-hour

ANIMUS

time frame. Those four keys looked like eight. He squinted and prayed for the silver key with the distinct scratch on it to show itself. That was the door key. He put the mark on it for times like this when he'd had one drink too many.

"You alright, baby?" purred his curvy companion. She pressed her large breasts against his back, reached around his waist, and grabbed his crotch. "You need some help with those keys?"

"Nah, I got it. But I can tell you this...what you got in your hand right now, ain't my keys."

"I disagree. I'm holding the key that will unlock my door."

Enis looked back at his companion and smiled; revealing a space vacated by a tooth that fell out a month earlier. The scotch had him seeing four large breasts and lips that seemed large enough to suck the chrome off an Amtrak train.

"I'm gon' tear you up."

"You promise?"

Enis squinted at the lock and stabbed at the keyhole with his key.

"Hurry up, baby. I need you to scratch my itch."

Enis bit his bottom lip and focused harder on the dancing keyhole. "There we go. Now, let's get in here so I can use the key you grabbed."

The door swung open. The woman shoved Enis in the back and he stumbled forward.

"Damn, baby. You ain't gotta push."

Enis turned in that uncoordinated way that most drunkards do and nearly pissed his pants. The dark-skinned, blonde hair beauty who'd gripped his manhood like it was a microphone she wanted to sing into, wasn't alone. Standing behind her were two mountain-sized men. The three of them looked like they were posing for a low budget album cover.

ANIMUS

"What the fuck is goin' on?" Enis asked, his slurred words left spittle dangling from his bottom lip. "What y'all doin' in my crib?"

"They're with me," said a voice from behind the two giants. The men—and woman—stepped aside and a stumpy black man wearing sunglasses, a leather jacket, jeans, and shiny black shoes, stepped forward. His Kangol hat was cocked on his bald head. The man reached into his breast pocket and pulled out a wad of cash and handed it to the woman.

"You set me up!" Enis said, looking at the woman in disbelief. "Booker, I know why you're here. I can explain."

"Enis, Enis, Enis…how you gon' explain embezzling ten thousand dollars of my money?"

"It was only eight grand, and I was gonna get it back to you." Enis shoved his hand into his pocket and pulled out some wrinkled bills. "This is about four hundred."

Enis handed the money to Booker. Booker gave the money to the woman. She shoved the money into her bra, kissed the vertically challenged man on the cheek, strutted out the door, and closed it behind her.

"The extra two thousand is interest. You're lucky I don't add more." Booker pointed at a chair next to the small dinette table. "Have a seat."

One of the men grabbed a chair and placed it in the middle of the floor. Enis was so focused on the man with the chair that he didn't notice the other man move behind him. The second man wrapped a tree trunk-sized arm around Enis' neck and squeezed. Enis clawed and squirmed, but to no avail. Once he surrendered, Mr. Thick Arms held him down in the chair. The other goon removed a roll of duct tape from his jacket pocket and bound Enis' wrist together.

"You ain't gotta do this, Booker. I've been doing the books for your night club for ten years. How much money I dun' helped you hide? How much money I dun' helped you keep in your pocket? You ain't gotta kill me over eight grand."

ANIMUS

"Who said I was gon' kill you? I just came here to ask why you did it and to give you the terms of my repayment plan." Booker sat on the faux leather sofa and strummed his fingers on the arm rest. "So, why did you feel the need to steal from me?"

"I don't know, bruh." The buzz Enis had when he arrived at his apartment vanished faster than the black widow that lured him into this trap. "I had a losing streak with the ponies. You know I'm good for it."

"How do I know that? You're robbin' Peter to pay Paul. But ya' see, you forgot one important thing...my name ain't Peter." He leaned forward. "I don't get robbed."

"I'm sorry, Booker."

"I'll bet you are." Booker shook his head pitifully. "E, you had to know this shit was gon' come back on you."

"I know I fucked up. Just tell me what I gotta do to make this right."

"For starters, you gon' repay me."

"Okay, I promise you, I'm gon' get every dime back to you. I just need some time."

"Where you gon' get ten grand from, E?"

"My son. He's doin' good in Dallas. I'm gon' call my son."

"Enis, Enis, Enis...you forgot that you told me your son don't even fuck with you. As a matter of fact, you told me your son hates your guts."

"I know I said that, but he'll come through for me."

"And how do you know that?"

"Because I got somethin' on him."

"You'd blackmail your own son to get yo'self out of trouble." Booker chuckled and looked at one of his henchmen. "That's some sick shit, huh bruh?"

"Sick," Mr. Thick Arms replied.

"Honestly, I don't give a shit how you do it, I just want my money back to me by..." Booker scratched his chin and looked up at the ceiling. "...today is the 26th, I'm gon' give you

16

ANIMUS

until two weeks from today. That's September 9th. E, if you ain't got my ten grand by September 9th, you know shit gon' get bad for you, right?"

Enis didn't answer. He just stared at the floor.

"Yo' this nigga act like he don't hear me." Booker craned his neck to see if Enis was awake. He nodded at Mr. Duct Tape. "Wake that ma'fucka up."

Mr. Duct Tape removed a knife from his back pocket. He pressed the button on the knife handle and a shiny blade appeared.

"I'm up man!" Enis shouted. "I hear you!"

"You might hear me, but I don't think you feel me."

Booker nodded at. Mr. Duct Tape. The man flashed a gold tooth smile and drove the blade into Enis' thigh. Enis unleashed a scream that was loud enough to wake the dead. Mr. Thick Arms slammed his baseball glove-sized hand over Enis' mouth to stifle the noise.

"I bet yo' ass is woke now," Booker said.

Enis nodded. His tears settled on the henchman's fingers.

"Ten grand."

Enis nodded.

"September 9th."

Enis nodded again.

"If you don't have my money by then, they're gonna find you floatin' in the Bonnet Carré Spillway. Do you understand me?"

Enis closed his eyes and nodded one last time.

"Good. I'm glad we can come to an understanding. By the way, if you try to skip town, I'm gon' find you. And when I do, I'm gon' kill you, find a way to bring yo' bitch ass back to life, and kill yo' ass again. So, I suggest you put whatever plan you've cooked up to screw over you son into action fast." Booker stood up. "Now, my man here is going to remove his hand from your mouth. If you yell, I'm gon' have my other man here fuck up your other leg. Is that what you want?"

ANIMUS

Enis shook his head.

Booker gave the signal and Mr. Thick Arms removed his hand. Mr. Duct Tape wiped the blade on Enis' shirt and then cut the duct tape to free Enis' hands. The three men left the apartment as calmly as they entered.

Enis fell to the floor and writhed in pain. The neighbors beneath him would often bang on the ceiling if he walked too hard, but now that he needed them to be nosy, they weren't. Surely, they heard him scream. They must've heard him flopping on the floor like a fish out of water. When five minutes passed and no one came to check on him, Enis realized he was on his own.

Enis crawled over to the sofa, leaving a trail of blood on the musty carpet, and managed to stand up. He hobbled into the bedroom and grabbed a belt from the closet. After fastening the belt around his upper thigh to slow the blood flowing out of his wound—a tactic he learned as a soldier and had the misfortune of utilizing on himself and fellow soldiers during Vietnam—he packed the wound with globs of Vaseline until the bleeding stopped. A thick gauze was used to cover the wound, but no sooner than he'd stopped the bleeding, the liquor he'd consumed did a number on his head. The headache that kicked in produced a pain that riveled the pain in his leg.

Enis' hands trembled as he worked a cellphone from his pocket and typed a text message:

I need 10K asap.
A reply came within seconds.
10K…are you serious? I don't have that kind of $.
Enis replied: **You think Rob will give it to me?**
The reply: ***You really asking me this? Why do you need that kind of $?***
Enis replied: **Long story. Explain later. If you talk to him for me, I'll make sure you're straight.**

ANIMUS

The reply took a while to come back. Enis grimaced and was about to type again when the response he'd been waiting for popped on the screen:

Let me see what I can do.

3

August 31, 2005/New Orleans, LA.
8:26 a.m.

Robert Sumina stood in front of his 60" wall-mounted television with his mouth parted and his eyes as wide as saucers. The scene on the television screen shook him to his core. So much so, that he could feel a tightness in his chest and queasiness in his stomach.

"Baby, you're standing in front of the television," Melody said. "Move over and turn it up."

Robert's arm raised robotically. He aimed the remote at the television and covered his mouth with his other hand while he stepped to the side, his six-four, muscular frame, seemingly in slow motion. Once he was no longer blocking

ANIMUS

Melody's view, he shoved his hands in the pockets of the gray jogging suit he wore and watched with amazement.

The roofs of houses stuck out from a thick blanket of murky water like the shrimp, sausages, and crabs that dance on the surface of a dark boiling gumbo. The wide range shot of the drowning city switched to a flustered white reporter wearing a green parka and baseball cap. He shouted his commentary with the hopes that his rehearsed soliloquy could be heard over the roar of the helicopter's buzzing propellers. This was the news event of a lifetime—the type of event that could earn a reporter an Emmy Award and catapult his career into the stratosphere.

"I'm Charles Deitrich, reporting live from high above the flooded Lower Ninth Ward area in New Orleans. I'll tell you this, never in my twenty years on the job have I seen this type of devastation to property, life, and the human spirit. We just flew over the levee breech and I...I'm in awe at the damage that has been done to this area. From the industrial canal to Caffin Avenue and from Caffin Avenue all the way to St. Claude Avenue, it looks like a muddy lake.

"From the looks of it, the water level appears to be hovering around the gutters of the few houses that remain standing. I estimate the levels to be between eight to ten feet. I've seen men paddling in canoes down what used to be Claiborne Avenue. At this very moment, we are flying over an area between Claiborne Avenue and Florida Avenue. I see people trapped on the roofs of their houses holding signs that say: HELP US!

"Folks, this is the most horr..." Dietrich paused for dramatic effect, "...horrifying thing that I've ever seen." Dietrich looked directly at the camera. With frown lines as deep as gullies carved into his forehead and knuckles that were bone white from gripping the microphone, he said with a shaky voice, "I don't know what government officials are listening to me at this moment. I don't know what bureaucracy is slowing

ANIMUS

down the search and rescue process. All I know is that these people need help. And they need help now!"

Robert sat on the sofa next to Melody. He placed his hand on her thigh and caressed it until she stopped fidgeting.

"I can't believe I'm seeing this," Melody muttered.

"I know. It's like something out of a movie."

"That's our old neighborhood. A decade ago, we lived in the same area they are flying over. That could've been us sitting on top of the roof."

"As stubborn as I used to be about leaving town when a hurricane came through, it definitely would've been us on top of the roof."

"How many people do you think have drowned already?"

"A lot."

Robert draped his arm around Melody and aimed the remote at the television. He changed the channel to CNN. The scene on that channel was just as terrifying.

"We have our on-ground reporter, Liza Frontier, reporting from the Louisiana Superdome," said the desk reporter. "Liza, can you give us an update on what's going on?"

"Yes, John," said a frail reporter. Her long blonde hair was pulled back into a ponytail. "I'm here on the terrace of the Louisiana Superdome, and as you can see, its chaos. We are two days removed from Hurricane Katrina touching down in the city, and thousands of refugees who failed to evacuate the city are stranded here at the place that the New Orleans Saints football team call home. Thousands of people are wandering around like zombies trying to figure out where they will call home when this is all over."

"They're not there because they wanna be!" Robert yelled. "When you're poor, you can't afford to evacuate the city every time a hurricane comes through; you'd be evacuating three or four times every year. Shit, most of those people are probably struggling to make ten dollars an hour. A lot of 'em don't even have cars—they catch the bus back and forth to work every day. If you don't have a car, how in the hell are you gon' just pack up and evacuate? Hell, even a lot of the people with cars can't afford to leave. You need money for gas, hotels, food, and all kinds of other miscellaneous stuff."

"Baby, those reporters don't see it that way," Melody said and used the balls of her hands to dab at the corners of her tear-filled eyes. "All they see are people who failed to leave the city when they knew a hurricane was headed straight for it. Those reporters from CNN and MSNBC aren't from Louisiana. They don't really understand how things are down there."

"I hear you, but I hate the way they are reporting it. If you gon' tell the story, tell the whole story. Most of those folks trapped in the Superdome are living from paycheck to paycheck; they barely have enough money to survive on a regular day." Robert's face scrunched and he stared at the reporter as if he could smell the stench surrounding her. "And why do they keep calling them refugees? They aren't from some foreign country trying to come to America to escape danger. They are American citizens trying to survive a catastrophe right here."

"Mayor Nagin has asked neighboring cities like Baton Rouge and Lafayette to send as many buses as they can spare to transport refugees out of the Superdome and on to Texas," Liza Frontier said. "In fact," she pointed out at Poydras Street; the camera followed the direction of her skeletal hand, "we can see dozens of tour buses lining up outside the Superdome now."

"Liza we've heard stories of violence at the Superdome. Can you confirm whether that is true?" asked the desk reporter.

"I sure can," Liza responded. "I've seen people arguing and fighting. As a matter of fact, I wanna let you hear from some of the people trapped here at the Superdome, so that you can get a better feel for what they are dealing with. Umm

ANIMUS

ma'am...ma'am, my name is Liza Frontier from CNN. Can I ask you a few questions?"

"Miss, unless you gon' tell me when we gettin' the fuck outta here, don't ask me no damn questions," barked a skinny black woman wearing a bonnet, tank top, shorts, and carrying a toddler.

"Uhh, yes...yes ma'am. I understand your anger." Liza looked at the camera. The distraught woman's scolding made the reporter's pale skin turn pink. Being the seasoned veteran reporter that she was, Liza pivoted as smoothly as the circumstances would allow. "Live interviews are always tricky. Considering the stress levels here in New Orleans, that young mother's reaction should be expected."

Liza looked around and walked toward a bearded white man leaning against the wall.

"Un-huh, you see she's goin' toward a white man this time," Robert said.

"She learned her lesson," Melody said. "She ain't about to approach another sista with a stupid ass question and get her face cracked again on national television."

"Sir, I'm Liza Frontier from CNN. Do you mind if I ask you a few questions about the conditions inside the Superdome?"

"You got a cigarette?" the disheveled man asked.

"Umm, no sir, I don't."

The man waved dismissively and walked away. Liza's face turned an even darker shade of pink.

"As you can see, these people are frustrated and confused. Children have been separated from their parents and...and it's just chaos. As my crew and I were making our way to this spot, we passed three people who appeared to be dead on the I-10 overpass. They were just lying there covered in blankets—their loved ones next to them crying and praying. It's...it's...," Liza struggled to wrangle her words, "...it's terrible."

ANIMUS

Liza was about to throw the broadcast back to the desk reporter but was saved by a black man who appeared to be in his mid-twenties.

"Say, lady! You wanna know what's happenin' in the 'Dome?"

"Umm, yes," Liza replied enthusiastically. "Yes, I would. But before you tell me what's happening in there, tell me who you are and what you've dealt with since the flooding started."

"Oh, my name is DeMarcus. I'm out here with my people, ya' heard me?"

"Yes, yes sir…I hear you." Liza said. Her complexion started to turn back into its original pale state once she saw an opportunity to salvage a disastrous reporting effort. "Tell me sir, how did you get here?"

"Man, I'm from out that third, ya' heard me?" DeMarcus posed for the camera like a rapper shooting a video and held up three fingers. "Calliope Projects, ya' heard me!" DeMarcus refocused on Liza and planted his right fist in the palm of his left hand while he spoke. "Man look…real talk, me and my people wasn't even tryin' to come here. We were gon' walk across the bridge to try to get to Gretna by my grandma house."

"You mean the Crescent City Connection?"

"Yeah, that big ma'fucka right there!" DeMarcus said as he pointed at the massive cantilever bridge that hovers over the mighty Mississippi River and tethers the city's east and west bank. "You know another way to get across the river?"

"Umm, no…no sir, I don't. Please continue."

"Maaan anyway, we was gon' head over there, but we heard Harry Lee had his boys locked and loaded, and turnin' people around and shit."

Liza withdrew the microphone from DeMarcus and spoke into it as she eyeballed the camera.

"He's referring to the controversial Sheriff of Jefferson Parish, Harry Lee, who has been accused of being a racist by

ANIMUS

members of the African American community here in New Orleans, although he too is a minority."

"Accused," Robert blurted out, "his ass been a racist since we lived there as kids. That's why those white folks in Jefferson Parish have kept him in office for two decades. He keeps the niggas from New Orleans at bay."

"Sir, it's my understanding that the Gretna Police Department, which is not run by Sheriff Lee, is patrolling the west bank side of the Crescent City Bridge."

DeMarcus shrugged. "Man, I don't know who's doing what. All I know is that people came runnin' back toward us sayin' the police firing rounds over people's heads and tellin' them to turn around and go back on the east bank." DeMarcus paused to light a cigarette and then continued to embrace his fifteen minutes of fame. "So anyway, we walked over here to the 'Dome because we heard this is where the buses gon' be lining up to take people away."

"When did you and your family arrive here, sir?"

"We got here yesterday."

"Can you look into the camera and tell America what you witnessed inside the Superdome?"

DeMarcus nodded and grabbed the microphone. Liza was determined to not release it—the first thing all reporters are taught—but she relaxed her arm enough to let DeMarcus control it while she held on for dear life.

"Man look, it's crazy in there. People crammed in there like sardines. The air conditioner ain't workin'. The toilets ain't workin'. People smearin' shit on the bathroom walls."

"Excuse me, are you saying feces is being smeared on the walls?" Liza asked.

DeMarcus scratched his head and frowned as if he'd gotten a whiff of a dead body.

"I don't know nothin' 'bout feces, but they definitely smearin' shit all over the bathroom walls." He clapped his hands. "Anyway…like I was sayin'…it's bad ya' heard me." He pointed down at his feet. "Look at my feet." The camera man

ANIMUS

zeroed in on his plastic bag covered shoes. "That's why we got plastic bags over our shoes. People tryin' not to step in piss and shit; or cut their feet on glass and crack vials."

"Excuse me, did you say crack vials…as in the kind used to carry drugs? Are you sure that's what you saw?"

DeMarcus looked at Liza quizzically and then glanced at his friend. "Bruh, she asked me if I'm sure I saw crack vials on the ground."

DeMarcus' friend shook his head pitifully, rolled his eyes, and took a drag of his cigarette.

"Miss, I'm from the 'hood. You really think I don't know a crack vial when I see it?"

"Yes, yes, you're right, sir. I stand corrected. Please continue."

"There really ain't nothin' left to say other than they need to hurry up and send the Marines or somethin' because people losin' their minds in the 'Dome. Last night, a dude jumped off the balcony."

"You mean someone committed suicide?"

"Yeaaah, but I ain't worried about him, he a grown ass man. If he wanna be weak and take a leap, that's on him. I'm worried 'bout the little kids in there. Mafucka's snatchin' up kids in there. That's why me and my boy stayed up all night watchin' my people, ya' heard me."

"Are you saying that kids are in danger inside the Superdome?"

"You got rapists, pedophiles, junkies, hookers…all kinds of people runnin' around in there. It's so bad that at night all the women gotta sleep with the kids close by them. While the kids and the women are sleepin', the men form a circle around them and stay awake through the night to keep the rapists from grabbin' the women and kids."

"Is it that bad, sir?"

"Are you white?"

"Well…yes, I am."

ANIMUS

"Alright then." DeMarcus glanced over at his friend again. "She thinks I'm makin' this shit up."

"That's what it sounds like, dog," said the chain-smoking friend.

"It's bad-bad," DeMarcus said to Liza. "Some people in there actin' a fool, but truth be told, you got a lot of people comin' together in there too. I saw people of all races protectin' each other. It's like skin color don't matter because everybody in there is in the same fucked up boat. I saw black women holdin' white babies. White women holdin' black babies. People just tryin' to look out for each other, ya heard me?"

"Well, sir, I appreciate you providing a firsthand account of what's going on inside the Louisiana Superdome. I hope you and your family can get to safety and away from this madness."

"Shiii...I'm an uptown soldier. We gon' make it, ya' heard me?" DeMarcus grabbed the microphone, looked at the camera, and held up three fingers. "I wanna say what's happenin' to my people in the 3rd Ward and that Lower Nine. And my man Kong out the 17th—Hollygrove standup. And last, I wanna shout out all my people from the 7th Ward and the St. Bernard project, ya heard me? Buck and Black...we gon' make it through this ya' heard me!"

Liza had to use both hands to wrestle the microphone away from DeMarcus. After he walked away, she tucked strands of rogue hair behind her ears, took a deep breath, and stared at the camera.

"And there you have it folks, a first-hand account from a man who has been inside the belly of the beast and survived to talk about it. Based on what that young man told us, things are worse inside the Louisiana Superdome than we imagined."

Robert turned the volume down on the television and looked at Melody. "Have you heard from your family?"

"I spoke to Kim last night. She and the boys are trapped in the Superdome. Her phone died while we were talking, but she did tell me that people were being put on buses and shuttled out of town. She said they were going to get on the bus that's taking people to Houston. She also mentioned something about a bus coming to Dallas—that's the one I told her to try to get on if she could. Honestly, I don't care which one they get on, I just want them to head this way. I told her to call me once she arrives in Texas."

"That girl is so stubborn."

"No more stubborn than you just said you used to be."

"I know. But when I see how crazy things are in the 'Dome, I just wish she would've left earlier and came here."

"I begged her to come, but she said she needed to work for as long as she could. You know she took that job as a security guard. They had her working the graveyard shift when they knew a damn hurricane was coming. By the time she got off, they'd shut down I-10 to Baton Rouge and announced that anyone who hadn't already evacuated had to stay and find a safe place to ride out the storm."

"Did you send her some money like I told you to?"

"Baby, I tried to, but she refused to take it. She is determined to make it on her own. Ever since Jalen died, she acts like she's got a point to prove. She'd rather work two full-time jobs and babysit on the side, than take money from me." Melody closed her eyes and bowed her head as if she were praying. Without looking up at Robert she asked, "Have you heard from your people?"

"Yeah, I talked to a couple of my cousins. They're safe in Georgia." Robert leaned back on the sofa and sighed. He affectionately rubbed Melody's back. "Don't worry, Kim and the boys are going to be alright. Once they get to Texas, we'll get them here. I hope she can get on the bus coming to Dallas, but even if she can't, I'm going to get them here. If I have to drive down to Houston and pick them up, that's what I'll do. I got enough room in the Escalade to fit at least six or seven people. We can cram their luggage in the back of the truck and strap anything that can't fit to the roof."

ANIMUS

"Thanks, baby. I want to go to the bank and get some cash out. I suspect a lot of people will be taking in friends and family from Louisiana. The ATM lines will probably be long."

"That's a good idea." Robert reached into his back pocket and pulled out his wallet. "I'll tell you what…give that cash you take out of the bank to Kim. Also, here is that new credit card I got last week. I was going to christen it this weekend by buying a new stereo system for the truck, but that can wait. This card has a four-thousand-dollar limit. Tell Kim to use it to get the big things they'll need—like bedroom sets for her and the kids."

"Thank you, baby."

"I'll take care of the boys."

"I can give them some of the cash I get from the ATM."

"Nawh, I'll deal with them away from you and Kim. They are three teenage boys who probably feel defeated and a little emasculated because they couldn't do more to save their things and help their mama. Just put a bug in Kim's ear and let her know I've got her sons."

Melody grabbed Robert and tried to hug the life out of him. "I swear, I don't know what I'd do without you. Thank you for taking care of my family."

"It's all good. Your family is my family. They can stay here for as long as they need to."

Melody wiped her tears and rested her head on Robert's firm chest. Her eyes closed as she imagined the fear that her sister and nephews were dealing with. The images emblazoned in her mind unleashed emotions that were as untamable as the flood water that breeched the rickety levees charged with protecting her hometown.

"I'm so scared for them," Melody whispered.

"It's gon' be alright," Robert said and kissed the crown of his wife's head. He figured that response was more comforting than what he was really thinking: *I just hope they can get on one of those buses. Because if not, they are screwed.*

4

While Robert and Melody struggled to maintain their composure in their posh 4,300 square foot, five-bedroom home, his younger brother, EJ, and his wife of six years, Darlene, were twenty minutes away in their 1,800 square foot house having a different experience. They watched the same gut-wrenching footage on a significantly smaller television that sat atop a particle board stand. And although they were equally stunned by the devastation Mother Nature levied on their hometown, their conversation about Hurricane Katrina and the anguish it created, was much different.

"I can't believe this," EJ said. "The President should've already done everything in his power to save those people."

"Like what?" Darlene asked with a glass of wine in one hand and a blunt in the other. "Ain't nothin' he can do from Washington, D.C."

ANIMUS

"You sound crazy. He's the President of the United States. He can get things done with one phone call."

"No, what the people in New Orleans should've done was evacuate the damn city."

"Dee, you know it ain't that easy to evacuate."

"It's easier than staying there and drownin'."

"It cost money to just up and leave town. Sometimes they get three or four hurricanes a year. Ain't nobody got that kind of money. If we were still there, we might've—"

"Got our asses out of town," Darlene interjected, her eyes rolling as deliberately as her neck. "I don't care what our money situation was looking like, we would've got the hell out of there. Some bills just wouldn't get paid this month. We would've used that money to get plane tickets, bus tickets, or rented a car to get the hell out of there."

A retort danced on EJ's tongue, but he kept it caged with his teeth and pressed lips. Darlene stood a hair above five feet tall, but she had the brashness and attitude of an MMA fighter. Arguing with her was the ultimate exercise in futility. If she won the argument, she wouldn't let him forget it. If she lost the argument, she would act like that pink bunny on that battery commercial—she'd keep going and going and going, until some portion of her flawed argument was accepted.

EJ pushed what he really wanted to say back down his larynx and gestured for his feisty wife to pass the blunt. Darlene took her sweet time, but eventually handed it over.

"Have you talked to your people since yesterday?" EJ asked and took a long drag before passing the blunt back.

"Yeah, I spoke to my aunt and cousins this mornin'. Honestly, I don't know how many of my family members are in the Superdome. The ones that were smart enough to leave are already safe in a hotel in Shreveport. They asked if they could come here since they're less than three hours away."

"Damn, you ain't tell me that," EJ collapsed the leg rest on his recliner and stood up. At a little less than six feet tall, he was the runt of the litter in his family. He was also a tad bit

ANIMUS

lazy; therefore, the jogging suit he wore didn't complement his physique. "I've gotta go make some groceries so we can be ready when they get here."

"No, you don't," Darlene said nonchalantly. "I told them not to come."

"Why?"

"Because they got money. They can stay in a hotel."

"But it's probably gon' be months before they get the flooding under control and open New Orleans back up. You know how much money they'll end up spending on a hotel?"

"Don't know and don't care."

"Dee, that don't make no sense. We've got two empty bedrooms here."

"So."

"What do you mean, *so*?"

Darlene took a long drag of the blunt and then dowsed the tip out in an ashtray. She tilted her head slightly and blew a plume of smoke from her mouth. The smoke swirled around the blades of the ceiling fan. She watched the mist for a second and then replied.

"I'll tell you what 'don't make no damn sense'," Darlene said and stared at EJ, "the fact that we've been married for six years and we're still leasing this raggedy ma'fucka. When we got married you talked me into leaving New Orleans and moving here, away from all my family, so we could have a *better life*. You also promised to buy me a house." Darlene scooted on the sofa until her back touched the cushions. She tucked her legs underneath her body, crossed her arms, and glared at EJ. "Now, you expect me to invite my family *here*? You gon' explain to them why I'm not livin' no better than I was in New Orleans?"

"This ain't about our house. It's about givin' your family some place to stay while they try to get back on their feet."

"No, this is about givin' them some place *decent* to stay while they get back on their feet."

ANIMUS

"No, this is about givin' them some place *decent* to stay while they get back on their feet. That hotel they're in is probably better than this dump." Darlene pointed in the direction of every area in the house that she had a problem with. "The damn toilet in the hallway doesn't work sometimes. The mice have a party in the kitchen every night. The roaches twerk on any piece of food you leave on the counter. And this old ass carpet stinks." She shook her head in disgust. "Nawh, my people ain't comin' here. They can stay at that hotel in Shreveport or wherever they wanna go, but I don't want them comin' here." After taking a sip of her wine, she continued. "I thought you were going to ask your brother for the money we need for a down payment for a new house."

"I didn't get a chance to."

"Well, when are you goin' to? I told you, I'm not stayin' here another year if you don't buy me a house like you promised."

"Dee, you know Rob is the tightest ma'fucka on the planet. I ain't never met somebody who makes as much money as him and just sits on it. Other than buying stuff for his house, he hardly spends money on anything."

"That's why you know he can spare a few thousand."

"I just told you not to worry about it. Just know that I got somethin' workin'."

Darlene sucked her teeth and slid off the sofa. EJ watched her walk toward the kitchen; his manhood stiffening with each seductive step she took. Even when he was annoyed at Darlene, that coke bottle figure of hers had a way of calming him down. Her chocolate legs were the perfect columns to keep an ass worth fighting over propped up.

"Girl, come here."

Darlene turned around and aimed those beautiful brown eyes of hers at EJ. She was sexy enough to bring a man to his knees and knew it. EJ visualized her naked and grabbed himself.

34

ANIMUS

"I don't know why you rubbin' your dick and lickin' your lips. You ain't gettin' none of this until you come up with a plan to move me into somethin' like your brother and his bougie ass wife live in."

"Rob owns several businesses. He can afford to buy Mel a house like that."

Darlene planted a hand on her hip—her way of saying "what's your point" without uttering a word. EJ smiled and gestured for her to come over. She sashayed over and stood in front of him. After shifting her weight to one side so that her left hip stuck out enough to make him drool, she folded her arms across her midsection.

"Baby, you know I'm gon' take care of you." EJ gripped her plump ass and buried his face in her crotch. "It's just taking a little longer than planned."

"A little longer than planned, huh."

"Yeah. But trust me, I'm gon' figure somethin' out."

"Well, while you're tryin' to figure somethin' out," Darlene said, the tips of her nails gently gliding along the back of his neck, "maybe I should be askin' your brother to buy me a house since he's the one with all the money."

EJ's groping stopped as fast as it started. He'd spent his entire life living in the shadow of his older brother. Robert left a legacy in high school sports that EJ struggled to match. It was Robert's name scrolled on the girl's bathroom stalls, not his. Robert made good grades, went to college, and earned a bachelor's degree from Southern University while EJ struggled to graduate high school. Whereas penny ante jobs awaited EJ post-graduation, Robert joined the military as an officer and served his country for eight years. And it was Robert who took the entrepreneurial leap at the age of thirty and made EJ, who was twenty-five years old at the time, one of the first hires at RTS Landscaping, the landscaping company he owned.

Ten years had passed since EJ received his first check signed by his more accomplished older brother. During that time, Robert opened RTS Janitorial Services and RTS Pool

ANIMUS

Cleaning. He wasn't a millionaire, but his annual income was in the high six-figures and EJ was still the younger brother riding his coattails. Which is why Darlene's snide remark pierced the fatty layer of EJ's beer belly like a dagger with a jagged edge.

EJ's fingers curled into a tight fist. He gritted his teeth. Before Darlene knew what happened, her underachieving husband leapt to his feet and clamped his hand around her throat. EJ pushed his loquacious wife backward until her back kissed the wall.

"Don't ever say no shit like that to me! You hear me?"

EJ's vice-like grip prevented words from escaping his flippant wife's mouth. Darlene was forced to respond with a slight bob of her head. When pools of water formed in her eyes and her lips quivered, he was convinced she'd gotten his point. He loosened his grip and watched her slouch, cough, and rub her neck.

Feeling like he'd recovered the masculinity snatched from him by Darlene's passive-aggressive comment, EJ glowered for a moment and then grabbed the blunt out of the ashtray. He could hear Darlene scamper away as he lit the blunt.

While savoring a long toke, EJ's head snapped back. Darlene stood behind him on the tips of her and pressed the blade of a butcher knife against his throat.

"Nigga, if you ever put your hands on me again, I swear, I'm gon' use this knife to cut yo' little pencil dick off when you go to sleep. Now...do you hear me?"

EJ nodded in the same terrified way Darlene had a few seconds earlier.

Darlene kept the blade pressed against EJ's neck until she was convinced that she'd made her point. Slowly, the petite vixen backed away. Once the possibility of being grabbed was gone, she turned and walked to her bedroom and slammed the door so hard that the frame creaked.

ANIMUS

EJ rubbed his neck. A layer of blood glazed his fingertips. He sucked the blood off his fingers, looked over at the bedroom, and shouted, "You crazy bitch!"

He plopped down on his favorite chair, yanked the lever, and reclined. As he looked up at the ceiling fan he thought about his predicament.

I did promise to get her a house. I really thought I would've had the money saved up by now. EJ bit down on his bottom lip and shook his head in disgust. *I'm gon' get that money...by any means necessary.*

5

September 3, 2005/McKinney, TX. 8:26 a.m.

The darkness that cloaked the city of Dallas and its surrounding suburbs surrendered its stranglehold once the sun arrived for work in the east. Rays of light leaked into the Sumina household through the window blinds and revealed the morose look on Melody's face. She was too worried about Kim and her three sons to sleep, so she stared at the ceiling as if it were one of the massive screens at the drive-in movie theater their father, Frank, took them to when they were kids.

At least one Friday every month, Frank would come straight home from his job at the post office, load up their station wagon with snacks, blankets, and cans of bug spray, and take her and Kim to the drive-in to see movies like: *Star Wars*, and *Raiders of the Lost Ark*. Watching action movies on screens as large as mountains was exhilarating and birthed her desire to become a screenwriter.

Melody studied journalism at Southern University to because it was a respectable career and it helped her learn the mechanics of writing, but once Robert's businesses took off, she quit her job as a journalist for the Dallas Morning News and focused solely on trying to write a spec script that someone in Hollywood would like. In ten years, she'd only managed to sell one script—that was never turned into a movie—but an upper middle-class lifestyle afforded her the luxury of patience.

In 1981, the old drive-in movie theater in Algiers vanished. Ten years later, her father joined their mother in heaven. And now, the city she called home was swallowed whole by a vengeful Mississippi River and the waters of Lake Pontchartrain.

All Melody had left, outside of Robert and her twin-girls: Faith and Hope, was Kim and her three sons: Jalen, Johnny, and Josh. As the oldest, Melody felt it was her job to protect them. She had every intention of doing just that, but first she needed to get her family to the place that would serve as their haven—her home.

Work-related stress, coupled with the anxiety caused by the hurricane, had taken a toll on Robert. The moment his head touched the pillow his eyes slammed shut. As was his routine, he draped his muscular arm over Melody's waist and remained in that position throughout the night.

Melody understood how hard her husband worked and his level of exhaustion, so she cautiously slithered out of bed. She put on her slippers and robe, grabbed her cellphone, and tip-toed out of the bedroom.

The kids were still upstairs sleeping. The house was quiet—too quiet. Melody turned on the television and flipped

ANIMUS

the channels to CNN to get an update on the current conditions in the Big Easy. While Ray Nagin, the cocky and controversial Mayor of New Orleans, gave a status report on the evacuation process, Melody decided to make a pot of coffee. When her cellphone buzzed and an unfamiliar number appeared on the screen, she pressed the red button and sent it to voicemail. The phone buzzed again before she could place a coffee pod into her Kuerig—it was the same number.

"Oh shit…that might be Kim!" Melody grabbed the phone. "Hello!"

"Melody, it's me!"

"Kim!"

"Yeah. I can't talk long. My phone still isn't charged, but the woman I'm sitting next to on the bus was nice enough to let me use her phone."

"Where are you?"

"We're at a rest stop somewhere in Texas. The bus driver stopped here to let people use the bathroom and stretch their legs."

"Which rest stop? What city?"

"I don't know. All I know is that we're supposed to arrive in some city called, DeSoto, in a little less than two hours. Do you know where that is?"

"Yeah. That's about an hour away from McKinney. Did he say where in DeSoto?"

"Hold on." Kim asked a man if he knew where they were being dropped off in DeSoto. "Yeah, I just asked a guy who is on the bus and he said they're dropping us off at the civic center in DeSoto. Do you know where that is?"

"No, but we'll find it. We'll be there by the time y'all get there."

"Okay. They're signaling for us to get back on the bus. We'll see you in two hours. Love you."

"Love you too, Sis."

ANIMUS

Melody double-timed back to the bedroom and burst through the door. "Baby, get up!"

Robert flinched the way he—and the other soldiers in his unit—had in Afghanistan whenever an improvised explosive device (IED) exploded in the wee-hours of the morning. His eyes ping-ponged around the room and he looked befuddled. After adjusting his body and craning his neck, he squinted until his beautiful wife came into focus.

"What's wrong, baby?" Robert asked, his voice as rough as sandpaper.

"Kim just called. She's on a bus headed to Dallas. They are supposed to arrive at the DeSoto Civic Center in two hours."

Robert glanced at the clock on the wall. "That puts them here around nine." He flipped the covers back and got out of bed. "Give me about thirty minutes to get cleaned up and dressed. We can leave here at around seven-thirty. It'll probably take us an hour and some change to get there." He paused to yawn and stretch. "We should beat her bus by about thirty minutes."

The Suminas' hit the road as planned, making the one-hour trek from the northern suburb of McKinney to the southern suburb of DeSoto in fifty minutes—thanks to adrenaline's influence on Robert's gas pedal foot. They stopped at a gas station a few blocks away from the civic center and picked up bags of chips, refrigerated sandwiches, candy bars, and drinks.

"Umm, you think you got enough junk food?" Melody asked sarcastically.

"Baby, we don't know how much they've had to eat or when they last had something to eat."

"You're right. I didn't even think about that."

ANIMUS

A crowd of people stood around their parked cars in the civic center parking lot. The scene reminded Robert of the way family members wait with great anticipation for their loved ones to be released from formation and allowed to mingle after graduating from basic training.

While waiting for the buses, people of all ages and races mingled and swapped horror stories about what they saw, heard, or suspected happened in New Orleans. The buzz of conversation created a cacophony that lasted until four double-decker charter buses were spotted in the distance.

"Here they come!" someone shouted.

Moments later, the buses pulled into the parking lot of the civic center. The sound of gravel crumbling under the weight of their mighty tires filled the air. The congregation cheered and shouted like the people on the bus were soldiers returning from war. In many ways they were. They'd survived a horror that rivaled that of many war-torn countries.

Those spectators who weren't cheering were crying or struggling to maintain their composure. But all equanimity was lost once the buses came to a stop and the doors opened. New Orleanians spilled into the parking lot as if they'd been poured out of a bucket.

Kim and her three boys were on the second bus. Robert and Melody spotted them first. Melody shouted and waved until Josh, Kim's youngest son, spotted his aunt. The boy tugged on his mother's arm and pointed.

Kim plowed through the crowd like a running back with the goal line in sight. When she cleared the last cluster of people, she leapt into Melody's arms and unleashed a wail that had simmered in her gut for days.

Seeing that their mother needed that moment with her sister, Jalen, Johnny, and Josh made their way to Robert and held their uncle as if he were the judge that had granted them pardons. Comparable scenes of anguish and elation could be seen throughout the parking lot. Four busloads of people. All with a shared pain and relief.

ANIMUS

The hour-long drive back to Robert's house was both thrilling and painful. When the boy's described the strategies they employed to protect their mother from hooligans in the Superdome, Robert could feel himself swelling with pride. He'd become good friends with their father, Jalen Sr., who was murdered while being carjacked just two years earlier. He knew that Jalen was in heaven beaming with pride as he watched his sons display the courage that he'd instilled in them.

Robert looked at the rearview mirror and saw Kim flash a prideful smile. Unfortunately, the moment was fleeting. The smile that unearthed her dimples flickered and vanished like the flame on a candle when she sniffed her armpits. The stomach-turning stench that oozed from their pores was a painful reminder that what they'd experienced would be with them for the rest of their lives.

Their body odors were so abhorrent that Robert had to wind down the windows during the ride back. He attempted to avoid embarrassing them by lowering the windows an inch or two every few miles, but his clandestine approach was exposed by thirteen-year-old Josh.

"You don't have to keep inching the windows down, Uncle Rob. We know we stink."

The remark ushered in some much-needed levity. The boys hurled playful insults at each other, but once the laughter subsided, the survivors of the worst natural disaster in U.S. history became glossy-eyed and pensive.

Melody reached back and grabbed Kim's hand. Robert, determined to be the rock his family needed, gripped the steering wheel at the two and ten position and fought back the tears that stung his eyes. It was the longest one-hour drive of his life.

6

September 3, 2005/New Orleans, LA.
9:19 a.m.

A gust of wind from the propellers of the helicopter tossed shingles around like they were confetti. The debris forced the people on the roof of the house to cover their faces while trying to grab the ladder tossed down to them. With reports of alligators in the area, a water rescue was ruled out. If the evacuees intended to place their feet on something other than a damp roof—that could collapse at any moment—they'd have to summon the strength needed to dangle from the ladder or wait for the next good Samaritan to row past in a canoe.

"Grab the ladder and hold on tight!" shouted the Coast Guardsman.

ANIMUS

Once the rescuer was confident that the evacuee had a firm grip of the ladder, the thumbs up signal was given to the co-pilot. The helicopter climbed like a pelican—the state bird—and flapped its massive metal wings until it touched down on a designated landing spot at the Louisiana National Guard campus two miles away.

Several 2.5-ton cargo trucks awaited evacuees at the National Guard campus. Civilians, most of whom had never been on a military installation let alone a military vehicle, looked dazed and confused while they were being herded on to the back like cattle.

Although it was four days after the flood waters turned the Lower Ninth Ward into a swamp, the water was still high enough to stretch the 15-minute drive to an hour. The shivering passengers watched in jaw-dropping amazement as the trucks moved at a snail's pace through the flooded streets.

At the peak of the evacuation more than ten thousand people were at the Superdome. Once President Bush activated federal resources, the crowd dwindled by the thousands each day. Even as the crowd dwindled, tents that were set up to meet the needs of the elderly and military veterans remained.

"Sir, come this way please!" shouted a female soldier dressed in BDU's. She wore sergeant rank on her collar and barked orders like being in charge was nothing new to her. She gestured for the skinny black man to come toward her. "I see you're wearing an Army cap, sir. Are you a veteran?"

"Yes," the man replied. He clutched the strap of the backpack slung over one shoulder. "I'm a Vietnam Vet."

"Thank you for your service, sir. My name is Sergeant Hood."

The man nodded his thank you.

Sergeant Hood grabbed the man by the crook of his arm and guided him to a table that was set up in the corner near one of the inoperable escalators.

"Sergeant Riles! This gentleman is a veteran. Please take care of him."

ANIMUS

Sergeant Hood gave the man a respectful pat on the shoulder and said, "Sergeant Riles is going to get you where you need to be, sir."

"Hello, sir, I'm Sergeant Riles." He pointed at the man's black cap with gold letters stitched on it. "I see you're a Vietnam Veteran."

"Uh, yeah."

"Well, thank you for your service, sir. Now, let's get you to safety. What's your name, sir?"

The man removed his cap and used his filthy t-shirt to wipe his brow. "Enis…Enis Sumina."

"Mr. Sumina, you seem to be limping. Do you need medical assistance?"

"I hurt my leg trying to climb to the roof of my apartment building," Enis lied. It seemed a more fitting excuse than admitting that a thug named Booker sicked two goons on him. "I'll be okay."

"We're getting veterans like yourself into VA facilities that can help you. We have different buses waiting to take people to various cities. But first, I need to know if there is a city you want to go to during this evacuation process. Maybe some place where you have family members who can pick you up from the VA Hospital in that city. I'm going to put you on the bus headed in the direction of your chosen city."

Enis' stare was as blank as a sheet of paper fresh out of the pack. His body was in the Superdome, but his mind was still on the roof he'd been plucked from. He made eye contact with the soldier sitting at the table in front of him, but images of dead bodies and nutria rats were all he could see. He'd spent two days swatting at the vermin with his rescue sign, branches, and pieces of gutter. The rodents were persistent. The more he swung the louder they squealed. Even with the noise surrounding him at that moment, all he could hear was the sound of those angry rats.

ANIMUS

"Mr. Sumina!" the soldier said. "Is there a city you'd like to go to? I need to know so I can put you on the right veteran designated bus."

"Umm...yeah, Dallas. I wanna go to Dallas."

"Do you have family in the Dallas area? Someone who can pick you up from the VA Hospital?"

"Yeah." Enis looked back at the line of veterans behind him. "My sons live in Dallas. One is a veteran. I wanna go there."

The unpleasant smell on the crowded bus was as bad as the one in the Superdome. Men and women ranging in ages from 20 to 75 sat shoulder to shoulder like slaves on ships during the Middle Passage. Some cried. Some rested their heads on the window and stared aimlessly out at the remnants of the worst hurricane in forty years. Most were asleep before the bus was out of the city limits.

When the bus crossed the Bonnet Carré Spillway, Enis thought about Booker's threat to toss him into it if he didn't return the money he'd stolen. Before he could linger on the thought of encountering Booker's goons again, the bus swayed and Enis' trance was broken.

Seated two rows behind the bus driver, Enis was crammed between a wrinkled white man who reeked of urine and a snaggletooth black man who smelled of whiskey. The white man was asleep with his head against the window and his mouth open. A string of drool that was thick enough to pull the bus they were on, swung like a pendulum from the man's bottom lip. Enis found himself staring at the drool, hoping it would remain the property of its owner and not get on him.

"What's happenin' brotha?" asked the black man sitting to Enis' right.

The man had one foot in the aisle and the other invading Enis' space. He wore a cap signifying he too had been

ANIMUS

in Vietnam and a soiled and tattered pea coat that made Enis itch just from looking at it. The only thing worse than the man's body odor was his breath.

Enis nodded, hoping the man would end the discussion with a greeting—he didn't.

"Man, I'm glad to be out of there. What part of the city you from?"

"9th Ward," Enis mumbled.

"I heard y'all had it bad over there. I live in the Seventh—a block off St. Bernard and Claiborne around Circle Food Store." The man took a swig of his bottled water. "I decided to ride the storm out with my older brother. Man, we moved up to the attic when the water came in the house. Thought we'd be safe up there. Shiii…that water started rising on our asses. Before you know it, we were using anything we could to try to knock a hole in the attic ceiling so we could climb on the roof. My brother got a bad arm and leg, so I was pretty much banging on that ceiling by myself. It took me a few hours to open a hole big enough for us to climb through." The man paused and stared at the aisle where his foot, clad in a brown tennis shoe that was once white, rested. His voice lowered and he started to sound like he was talking to himself. "I managed to squeeze through the hole in the roof, but my brother…my brother couldn't make it. I tried to pull him up, but I couldn't do it. I'm a buck fifty soaking wet. My brother weighed a good two-fifty." The man took another swig of his water. "He got stuck. Can you believe that shit? He got tired of trying and let my hand go. He slid back down in the hole. It was like the water swallowed him up."

When the man came out of his stupor, all three of the passengers across the aisle were looking at him. Their eyes were glued to him the way children become fixated on the adult telling them a bedtime story.

Enis listened too, although he pretended to not be interested. He instinctively knew the expectation was that he'd serve up a horror story to match, but he didn't comment.

ANIMUS

After a few seconds passed, the man looked at Enis and said, "This bus is heading to Houston and then on to Dallas. Where you going?"

Enis wiggled his shoulders to get more comfortable in his seat, hugged the backpack, and closed his eyes. Without looking at his loquacious neighbor he replied, "I'm going to sleep. I'm gon' need you to shut up and do the same."

By five o'clock that evening, the VA Hospital was a madhouse. The normal population was doubled when the Louisiana natives arrived. The hospital staff worked feverishly to accommodate the new arrivals but trying to calm the excited crowd was a waste of time.

The first thing Enis wanted to do was recharge his cellphone. He'd had the presence of mind to put on a water-resistant jacket when the flood waters forced him on to his roof. The jacket had pockets inside with zippers. The compartment enabled him to keep his phone dry but couldn't keep the battery from dying.

Enis surveyed the crowded waiting room and spotted a man sitting in the corner using a wall outlet to charge his phone. There was a space next to the wall that was wide enough for a person to stand, so Enis commandeered it before someone else did.

"You from New Orleans?" Enis asked the chubby man.

"Yeah, I from the 8th ward off Elysian Fields; around Brother Martin. What about you?"

"9th Ward," Enis replied and sat down with his knees pressed against his chest. "I'm just glad they found me."

"Tell me about it. I was in my house and that water started rising. I thought I was gon' die. Suddenly, some white men in a canoe came by and was yelling through my front door. I made my way to the front of the house and climbed my fat

ANIMUS

ass in that boat before they could ask if I needed help." The man looked around. "It's crazy in here, huh?"

"Yeah, but it beats being stuck on top of your house."

"I hear ya', baby." The man scanned the waiting room again. "I gotta piss like a racehorse. I wanna use the bathroom, but I don't wanna take my phone off the charger. I'm tryin' to get some juice so I can call my daughter. I need her to come and get me the hell outta here."

"Man, if you gotta use the bathroom, go ahead. I'll watch your phone. The bathroom is around the corner and at the end of the hall. But I'm tellin' ya' now, the line is long as hell."

The man sighed and shrugged. "It's either get in that line or piss in this chair." The man checked his phone one last time. "I appreciate ya', bruh. I'll be back."

The man side-stepped a few veterans sitting in the middle of the floor and wobbled around the corner. Enis waited a few seconds and then snatched the charger out of the man's phone and charged his own. It took a minute for his phone to come to life, but when it did, he immediately dialed a number.

"Yeah, I'm in town. I'm at the VA Hospital." he said. "I cut my leg, so I'm gon' see a doctor so they can clean it up before it gets infected. There are so many people in here, it might not be until tomorrow before I get to leave. As soon as they cut me loose, I'm headed that way."

7

According to Maslow's Hierarchy of Needs, a human's most basic needs are physiological: air, water, food, shelter, and sleep. Therefore, it should come as no surprise that the behavior of some of the evacuees in the Superdome was deplorable. The stench-filled air was suffocating. Water and food were limited. And the mayhem inside and outside made sleeping close to impossible.

While Kim and her boys washed off the remnants of the worst three days of their lives, Robert retrieved some old jogging suits he'd outgrown from the attic. He laid them out in one of the two guest bedrooms for Jalen. The boy was nearly six feet tall and would have no problem wearing them. Johnny and Josh were a little smaller, so he grabbed a couple of t-shirts and shorts with draw strings for them. The clothes made them all look like ragamuffins, but they'd have to suffice until a trip to Walmart could be made.

ANIMUS

Melody and Kim both wore a size 6, so Melody placed a few outfits in a separate guest bedroom for her sister. Clean and clad in fresh clothing, the family of four was able to relax and move around without wondering if their presence triggered the gag-reflex of everyone around them.

"Y'all come on in here and eat!" Melody shouted.

"That smells good, Auntie," Johnny said.

"It's cabbage," Faith said.

"No, it's not. It's collard greens," Hope said. "You don't even know the difference between cabbage and collard greens."

Kim smiled and hugged Faith. "Don't feel bad, baby. I couldn't tell the difference either when I was your age."

Everyone sat down. Robert noticed how Jalen, Johnny, and Josh stared at their plates the way a lion sizes up its prey, so he kept his prayer short and sweet.

"Heavenly Father, we thank you for the blessings you've bestowed on us and this food you've allowed us to receive. We especially thank you for getting our family here to us safely. In Jesus name, Amen."

There was a collective "Amen", and then the sound of forks scraping against plates dominated the room. It was music to Melody and Robert's ears.

"Girl, I forgot how good you can cook," Kim said as she savored a piece of cornbread.

"Yeah, this taste good, Aunt Mel," Jalen said.

Johnny and Josh nodded their approval while cramming clumps of greens in their mouths. They all scoffed down the food like parolees eating their first home cooked meal in years.

"Thanks," Melody said. "Y'all can have as much as you want. I made a huge pot of greens."

"Good," Josh said. "I got tired of eating potato chips everyday while we were in the 'Dome."

"Y'all didn't eat regular food when y'all were in the Superdome?" asked Faith.

52

ANIMUS

"They couldn't eat regular food," Hope answered. "They didn't have kitchens in there."

"No, baby, we didn't eat food like this." Kim said and bit into her cornbread. "Even if they did have kitchens available, the food wouldn't have tasted like this. Your mama has been cooking ever since we were y'all age. After our mama died, your mama used to cook dinner for me and your grandpa at least three times a week. And she was just around ten or eleven years old."

"Did mama teach you how to cook, Tee Kim?"

"No, baby. Your mama was mean. Since she was two years older than me, she thought she was the boss of me."

"I was," Melody said.

"She used to make me do my homework while she cooked."

"First of all, I wasn't mean. Your auntie was hard-headed. All she wanted to do after she got home from school was eat snacks and watch cartoons. Secondly, don't make it sound like I was cooking meals like a chef. I cooked scrambled eggs and toast twice a week and spaghetti with meatballs once a week."

"But it was good," Kim said. She reached over and grabbed Melody's hand. "Your mama always took care of me."

"Stop it, you gon' make me cry," Melody said.

Random conversations continued to bounce around the table while everyone finished eating their meals. The kids all swapped jokes and laughs. The cousins hadn't seen each other since Mardi Gras—six months before the terrible storm—and the sound of their laughter brought joy to the hearts of their parents.

Robert chimed in whenever he could by asking the boys questions about their studies and athletic endeavors. Their smiles were proof that the joy they'd lost in the flood waters was recoverable.

While the kids conversed, Melody, Robert, and Kim spied each other with anxious eyes. They all realized that Kim had lost everything she owned: car, house, furniture, clothes, important documents—everything. Life had tossed the single mother a curve ball that most major leaguers couldn't hit. No words were said between the three of them, but they knew that massive potholes and setbacks awaited Kim on the road to recovery.

Melody noticed her sister fighting back tears. She gripped Kim's fingers and mouthed: *We got you*. Kim forced a smile and mouthed: *I know*.

Once their bellies were full and the hour of fellowship was complete, Kim and her boys adjourned to their assigned bedrooms to satisfy their last physiological need—sleep.

Three hours can pass faster than the speed of sound when you are sleep deprived. The king-sized sleigh bed that Kim slept on welcomed her into its clutches and refused to let go. With its six hundred thread count sheets and Layla Hybrid mattress, that felt as if it was stuffed with clouds, her aching muscles received the attention they so desperately needed.

It took Kim a moment to realize where she was once she awakened. She rested her head on the headboard, yawned, and stretched so hard that her body spasmed. The clock on the nightstand read 7:43 PM.

I can't believe I've been asleep for nearly three hours, she thought.

Kim got out of bed and staggered over to the bedroom where her boys slept. The boys weren't there, but there was no doubt they had been. The beds were unmade and there were clothes sprawled on the floor.

"Hey, Sis," Kim said as she entered the living room.

"Hey, sleepy." Melody replied.

"Girl, I can't remember the last time I slept that good. I'm taking that bed with me."

ANIMUS

"That bed ain't got nothin' to do with it. You were mentally and physically exhausted."

"Yeah, I guess you're right." Kim curled up on the sofa next to Melody. "Where is everybody?"

"The girls are up the block at a sleep-over."

"Where are my big-head sons?"

"Out galivanting with their big-head uncle. Rob felt they needed to get out, so he took them to Walmart. He gave each of 'em one hundred dollars so they could buy whatever they want."

"Aww, he didn't have to do that."

"Girl, you know how Rob feels about those boys. They are the sons he never had. He wanted to give them their own money. He said it's a man thing and we," Melody pointed at herself and Kim, "wouldn't understand."

"Baaaby, you got yourself a winner."

"Trust me, I know."

"Well, I hope they enjoy their little shopping spree because when they get back, they got some cleanin' to do. I just looked in that bedroom and they left it a mess."

Melody waved dismissively. "Girl, don't worry about that. Ms. Gloria will be here on Monday to clean up."

"Oh yeah, I forgot about your *maid*."

"For the record, we don't call her a *maid*. She's just a person who comes twice a week to clean up. And don't forget, Robert wanted her here more than me. He is determined to keep his promise."

"Well, the woman's son did save Rob's life."

"Yeah, I know. The day before Oscar died, Robert promised him that he'd take care of Ms. Gloria so that she wouldn't have to go back to Mexico. Robert offered to just pay her like she was on his payroll, but she's a proud woman. She insisted that she work for her money."

"Shit, you're complaining, but I wouldn't be." Kim looked around the spacious living room. "This is a lot of house to try to keep clean."

ANIMUS

"Trust me, I'm not complaining. She's been with us a few years, so I'm used to her. I was kind of in my feelings when she first started, but once Robert assured me that he was doing it to honor his army buddy, I learned to get used to it. Besides, the girls love her. She's kind of nosey, but she's nice."

"Well, count your blessings."

"I do. I count them every day." Melody adjusted her body on the sofa so that she could face Kim. "Speaking of blessings, Robert and I wanna be a blessing to you."

"Mel, y'all don't have to—"

"Hush." Melody lifted her hand. "You don't tell us what to do with our money." She lowered her hand slowly. "As I was saying before you rudely interrupted...Robert and I have talked. We know you've lost everything, but we kind of see this as a blessing in disguise. New Orleans is a rough city. We were thinking that this might be an opportunity for you to relocate here permanently."

"Mel, I—"

"Let me finish please!"

Kim threw up her hands in surrender.

"You can't deny that the quality of life is much better here. Your boys would get a private school level education at these public schools. Hell, the high school they'd go to has a campus that's damn near the size of Dillard University. These kids out here are exposed to stuff like horticulture and aeronautics in high school—the type of stuff that only the kids in New Orleans who go to public schools like Ben Franklin or Catholic Schools like Jesuit, get exposed to. No gunshots. No armed robberies. None of that stuff."

"I get it, Mel, but let's keep it real, I can't afford to live in McKinney. The rent here for a decent three-bedroom apartment starts at twelve hundred dollars."

"You can buy a house. The mortgage would probably be a little less."

"Mel, the houses in McKinney start at two hundred-fifty thousand. I couldn't qualify for a home on what I make.

ANIMUS

Shit, as of right now, I'm unemployed. I couldn't qualify to buy a cardboard box."

"Yeah, but—"

"Un-uh, now you let me finish," Kim said and held up her hand. "They are already announcing that FEMA will be releasing funds soon. I'm gon' be outside that distribution center here in McKinney on Monday morning to get my check and a housing voucher. I'm going to get a furnished apartment or a house that is for rent, and me and my boys will stay here in McKinney until they reopen New Orleans. I get what you're saying about the quality of life here, but I'm going to get my little house in New Orleans rebuilt. I know it ain't all of this," Kim waved her hand like a game show host, "but it's mine. I worked two jobs to buy it and I intend to get it back."

Melody looked disappointed, but she nodded to show she understood.

"Come here, girl," Kim said and leaned in to hug her big sister. "I appreciate you; I really do. But if I wanted to relocate to McKinney or any place here in the Dallas area, I would've done it a long time ago. It's nice out here, but—"

"But you prefer to live in a city where there hasn't been any new construction in decades. Kim, the same potholes that were in the streets when we were kids still exist. There are damn near three hundred murders a year. You've got to live in Metairie to avoid getting mugged. Everything they do there is ghetto. The Zulu Ball is the most formal event black folk get to go to, and you have to bring your own damn food to that."

Kim pondered Melody's comment for a moment and smiled. "Yeah...that's about right."

Melody shook her head. She'd tried for close to a decade to get Kim to move to Dallas, but to no avail. She figured the Hurricane Katrina evacuation was just the external force she needed to win her kid sister over, but she was clearly wrong.

"Mel, what can I say...I'm a New Orleanian 'til I die." Kim shrugged. "Don't get me wrong, Dallas is a beautiful city."

ANIMUS

"Yes, it is."

"No argument here."

"But?"

Kim grimaced. "Dallas is like a beautiful salad bowl—it's shiny, expensive, and don't have a scratch on it. But the salad ain't got no dressing and taste like shit. Now, New Orleans," her voice elevated in excitement, "is the raggediest salad bowl you've ever seen. It's all dented. Ain't got no shine to it. If you put it on the counter, it wouldn't stop wobbling." Kim snapped her fingers and rolled her neck. "But baaaby…inside that bowl is the best damn salad you've ever tasted in yo' life."

Melody smirked.

"Heifer, you know I'm tellin' the truth. Y'all got all these nice suburbs with big houses. Y'all got your fancy high schools and big shopping malls. Still, it ain't nothin' but a predominantly white city with no culture."

"There is culture here."

"Stop it. When was the last time you heard somebody say they were going on vacation to Dallas?" Kim crossed her arms and cocked her head. "You haven't. You know why? Because there ain't no culture here—just a bunch of trust fund babies and expensive shit. We got enough culture in New Orleans to lend y'all. You gon' tell me you don't miss getting up at any time of night, any day of the week, and going to Café Du Monde to get some beignets."

"I don't."

"What about going to the drive thru and buying a daiquiri that'll knock you on your ass and then driving past the police while drinking it and not have to worry about getting pulled over?"

"I don't drink daiquiris."

"Oh, I forgot, you're miss high-society now. You don't miss Mardi Gras?"

"Nope. Too many people. Too much crime. And too much noise."

58

ANIMUS

Kim used the back of her hand to feel Melody's forehead. "Baaaby, something is definitely wrong with you."

"Ain't nothing wrong with me," Melody said and swatted away Kim's hand. "Something is wrong with you."

"Well, somethin' jus' gon' have to be wrong with me because I like fun stuff like Mardi Gras, Essence Festival, Bourbon Street, going to Saints games, or checking out live jazz bands every night of the week if I want to. Do y'all have jazz clubs here?"

"I guess so."

"You guess so," Kim mocked. "Sis, I like my live music, and I don't wanna have to wait until the weekend to hear some."

"But ya' see Kim, that's the problem. Everything you're naming centers around partying. There is more to life than partying."

"And there is more to do in New Orleans than party. There is more black history back home than here. New Orleans has three HBCU's. How many HBCU's are here in Dallas?"

"I believe Paul Quinn College is the only one," Melody mumbled.

"Un-huh. Six million people in this city and only one HBCU. Can y'all visit actual plantations here and see how black folk were treated during slavery? Or take a steamboat ride down the Mississippi River and see the route runaway slaves took to get to freedom? Do y'all have a historical sight like Congo Square—the only known place in the south where slaves were allowed to gather and have parties on Sundays?"

"No."

"That's another culture point for New Orleans," Kim said and made the check sign in the sky.

"Alright, alright, I get it," Melody said. "You can't get the N.O. out of your system."

"And I don't want to. The minute they open the city back up, I'm gon' be right back down there." Kim stretched to get rid of the residue of sleep that clung to her faculties.

ANIMUS

"Besides, I can't stay here long because y'all don't have enough seafood restaurants. Every other restaurant here is Tex-Mex. You know the only Mexican food I eat is a taco."

"We have seafood restaurants here."

"Child please! The closest thing to a decent seafood restaurant here is Pappadeaux's—and they fakin' it. Got all that New Orleans decor and we both know you can't find a Pappadeaux's restaurant within three hundred miles of New Orleans. They'd get run out of business with that average food and those high ass prices."

"You got a point there."

"I know I do."

Melody sighed. "Girl, what am I gon' do with you?"

"Keep lovin' me just the way I am and stop trying to make me feel bad about loving the place I came from." Kim gripped Melody's hand. "Mel, just because a place is newer and shinier, don't mean it's better."

"Well, since I can't talk you into relocating at least let us help you get back on your feet." Melody held up a finger. She grabbed her purse and pulled out a wallet. "We want you to use this credit card to buy whatever you need: kitchen supplies, bathroom supplies, a new bedroom set for you and the boys. Anything you might need to get your newly renovated house looking straight when you move back home. You can leave whatever you buy here in the shed in the backyard. The card is brand new and there is a four-thousand-dollar limit on it."

Kim stared at the credit card like it was a court summons and she was being served. The zest that was present seconds earlier when she talked about New Orleans dissolved like dust in the wind. Suddenly, she burst into tears and buried her face in her hands. Her body slowly slumped over until her head rested in Melody's lap.

"It's alright, baby," Melody whispered. "Let it all out. Even when you're finish crying, I'm gon' still be right here."

8

September 4, 2005/Dallas, TX.
4:04 p.m.

The intoxicating scent of brownies perfumed the Sumina household. Chattering kids sat on bar stools around the massive kitchen island. Their lips were covered in vanilla ice cream and chocolate. As usual, Hope and Faith talked incessantly—the trademark of ten-year-old girls—while their male cousins consumed scoops of ice cream and brownies at a record pace.

The adults sat in the living room and sipped wine. Talk of the trauma in the Superdome had subsided. They all seemed to be exhausted by the disturbing recounts, so they focused on

ANIMUS

lighter topics. The television was on, but the volume was so low that they couldn't have heard it if they tried.

"Josh, take your time, boy!" Kim shouted. "You act like I ain't never make brownies for y'all."

"Leave that child alone and let him enjoy his food," Melody said.

"She's just jealous she can't eat it like they do," Robert said and chuckled.

"You're doggone right I'm jealous," Kim said and squeezed her own thigh. "If I look at ice cream too long, I gain weight."

"I know that's right," Melody said.

"And you might wanna leave me alone," Kim said to Robert.

"Why? What did I do?"

Kim peered back at the kids and then lowered her voice as she leaned in to chastise her brother-in-law. "Why did you buy them all of those clothes?"

"Because I'm grown. It's my money. They are my nephews. And I can do whatever I wanna do because you ain't my mama."

Kim tossed one of the sofa pillows at Robert.

"Child, he tells me the same thing," Melody said.

"Seriously, Rob, I appreciate you lookin' out for them, but they don't need to be spoiled."

Robert finished off his drink and planted his elbows on his knees. He leaned forward so that only Melody and Kim could hear him.

"That's where you're wrong. Those boys needed to feel like men right now more than ever. I gave each of them one hundred dollars so that they could buy whatever they felt like they needed. I told them that while they're here, they had chores, and they're going to come to work with me every day."

"How are you going to get any work done with them with you?" Kim asked.

ANIMUS

Robert looked at Kim as if she was an alien. "Sis, I'm the boss. I don't work, I delegate."

"Exxxcccuse me," Kim said. She and Robert slapped high-five. Kim rocked back and looked at her sons. They seemed normal again. She looked at Robert. "Thank you for being the father-figure they need."

Robert nodded, winked, and said, "You're welcome."

The doorbell chimed. Robert was about to stand up, but before he could get to his feet, Faith leapt off her stool and raced out of the kitchen. "I got it! I got it!"

"I don't know why that child acts like she's losing her mind when the doorbell rings." Melody looked at Robert. "Since you and the boys had y'all little outing today, us girls goin' out tomorrow for some *girls* time."

"That's right," Kim said. "We're all going to get mani-pedis, have lunch, and do some shopping. And we expect this house to be spic-and-span when we get back."

Robert tossed the sofa pillow back at Kim.

"Faith, who's at the door?" Melody shouted.

"Uncle EJ!"

"Well don't leave him at the door. Y'all come inside."

The front door slammed. Faith shot past the living room and reclaimed her seat at the island. The other kids didn't pay her any attention when she left so they were oblivious to her return.

"Hey, what's up y'all," EJ said.

"Hey, brother-in-law," Melody replied.

EJ hugged Melody and looked at her sister. "Kim, Kim, Kim. Giiiirrl, you get finer every time I see you."

"Hey, EJ." Kim stood up to give him a hug, but before they embraced, she warned him. "Don't say nothin' crazy or try to touch my butt. My kids are right over there."

"I promise, I won't," EJ replied with a devilish grin. "Damn you smell good. Feel good too. When you gon' be my woman."

ANIMUS

EJ's flirting with Kim had become so commonplace that no one paid any attention to it. He was the fly that buzzes around the picnic table and Kim's hand was the fly swatter that had successfully kept him at bay for over a decade.

"You can't help yourself, huh?" Kim said and playfully punched his chest as she backed away. "I'll be your woman when you no longer have a wife."

"I didn't know you was coming this way," Robert said and gave his brother some dap.

"You know I was gon' make it over here to check on Kim and the kids." EJ looked over at the boys. "What's up fellas!"

"Hey, EJ!" shouted the boys in unison.

"Have a seat," Melody said.

EJ didn't move. Instead, he rubbed his hands together. Robert recognized that gesture as his brother's nervous tick.

"What's wrong?" Robert asked.

"Is everything okay?" Melody placed her wine glass on the coffee table. "You look nervous."

"Umm, I'm not staying long. I came to see Kim and the boys, but I also came to drop something off."

"What?" Robert asked.

EJ craned his neck toward the front door and waved someone over.

All eyes shifted from EJ to the figure that emerged from the hallway—it was Enis. His ripped sullied shirt clung to his body. His left pants leg was stained with blood from his thigh to his knee. The white tennis shoes he wore were the color of oatmeal. And a cloud of funk hung over him like the Pig-Pen character from the Peanuts cartoon.

Robert hopped to his feet like a soldier when a Drill Sergeant enters a room.

"What the fuck are you doing here?"

Robert tried to keep his voice low but failed miserably. Like an old EF Hutton commercial, all activity in the Sumina household ceased. The kids looked dumbfounded with their

ANIMUS

spoons hovering around their mouths as if they'd been zapped with a freeze ray.

"Babe, who is this?" Melody grabbed Robert's elbow.

Robert's desire to charge Enis was high and his ability to control his composure was at an all-time low. He placed his hand on his head, just above his forehead, and brought it down slowly as if Enis would somehow be gone when the act was complete—he wasn't.

Robert glared at EJ and without moving his lips asked: *Nigga, have you lost your fucking mind?*

EJ replied with his eyes: *Don't kill me. He made me do it.*

The room was quiet enough to hear an ant peeing on cotton. True to form, Faith broke the silence with one of her patented untimely questions. "Daddy, who is that?"

Everyone in the room, except EJ, appeared eager to hear the answer to the question. Robert didn't reply, but his non-verbal communication spoke loud enough to wake the dead. Those long fingers of his curled into tight fist. The muscles in his forearm twitched. Veins squirmed in his neck like worms clamoring to be set free. When he bit down on his bottom lip, Melody squeezed his arm.

"You need to get the hell out of here," Robert growled.

"Daddy!" Faith called out. "Who is that man?"

The uninvited guest took a step toward the kitchen island.

"Hey, baby, my name is Enis Sumina, Sr. I'm your daddy's, daddy."

9

Kim was the first person to speak up after Enis introduced himself. While the other adults in the room stared at each other like gunfighters waiting to see who'd draw their weapon first, she astutely recognized that the "grown folk" conversation which was about to take place would be too heavy for the adolescent ears around them.

"Kids, y'all gather up your ice cream and let's go on the patio." Kim snapped her fingers and pointed at the back door to expedite the process.

"But my ice cream is gonna melt outside," Faith said.

"I'm not asking you, young lady, I'm telling you...grab your ice cream and let's go out back."

The kids gathered their bowls and filed out the back door. Kim was right behind them prepared to coral the stragglers. Before closing the patio door, she looked back at her sister and hoped the situation wouldn't be combustible.

ANIMUS

That wish was wasted because before the door could close Robert unleashed his wrath.

"Why in the fuck would you bring him here?" Robert shouted.

If looks could kill, EJ would have needed a coroner.

"He lost everything in the storm," EJ said and took a step backward when he realized he was within striking distance of his irate brother. "He needs some place to stay."

"Then you should've brought him to your house!"

"Man, I wanted to, but Darlene ain't havin' it. She says my house ain't "company" worthy. She won't even let her own family members come."

"That ain't my problem!" Robert looked at Enis. "You need to get the fuck out of my house."

"Son, I realize I'm not your favorite person, but I really don't have anywhere to go. I would've got a hotel room, but the little money I have would run out in a week. If you'll just let me stay here for at least a week or two until I can figure some things out, I promise I'll never come back around. Please son, this will really help me out."

Robert moved so close to Enis that they could smell each other's breath. In that split second, his thoughts raced back thirty years when he was as helpless as David and his father appeared as formidable as Goliath. Back then, when Enis spoke the ground shook, the walls rattled, and time stood still. Robert remembered the times when even the thought of incurring his father's wrath made him urinate in his pants. But those days were three decades old. Now, all he saw before him was a man who was close to four inches shorter than him and appeared pitiful.

"I wouldn't piss on you if you were on fire. Now get your smelly ass out of my house before I throw you out."

"Rob, he's our dad," EJ said.

"And you get your shady ass out of here too! You know I don't fuck with him."

ANIMUS

"Honey, you're scaring the kids," Melody whispered and grabbed Robert's arm.

Robert could see his daughters looking at him through the window.

"Baby, let me talk to you for a moment." Melody tugged at her husband, but Robert's body was as stiff as a concrete column. "C'mon, baby, let's talk in the bedroom."

Robert gave ground and walked toward their bedroom. Melody held up a finger and gestured for Enis and EJ to stay put. She followed Robert into the bedroom and closed the door.

"I can't believe EJ brought that bastard here!" Robert paced from one end of the four hundred square foot bedroom to the other. "I'm about ready to put hands on his ass too."

"Alright, alright, just calm down for a second!" Melody rubbed her forehead and tried to gather her thoughts. "Before anybody gets tossed out, we need to think about this." She started pacing too. "I'm shocked your dad is here in our house. I mean, I knew he was alive, but all these years we've been together, I've never met him. You've always treated him like he was dead…and now he's here."

"That's because he's been dead to me." Robert quit pacing. "I told you all of the horrible things he did to me and my mother."

"Yes, you told me he was physically and verbally abusive, but damn Rob, he's here in the flesh. This is freakin' me out."

"Like I said, he's been dead to me."

"Yeah, but your lie affects more than just you, babe. I went along with your lie to keep the peace. Now I feel like shit for doing it. We've been telling our daughters their grandfather died in combat during the Vietnam War. How do you think those kids are feeling right now? I'm sure they're confused as hell right now. Shit, I'm confused as hell right now."

"Look, I can't argue with you about that. I shouldn't have pressured you into telling them he was dead. I'll talk to the girls and apologize to them later. But for now, that ma'fucka gotta get out of my house."

Robert set his sights on the bedroom door and was about to plow through it, but Melody stepped into his path and folded her arms.

"You ain't goin' nowhere?"

"Mel, move out of my way."

"Or what…you gon' put your hands on me the way he used to put his hands on your mother?"

Young boys who witness domestic violence either grow up to be abusers or they detest the thought of even appearing to be capable of such cruelty—Robert was the latter. He prided himself on being able to look anyone in the eyes and say that he'd never as much as raised a finger in violence toward a woman.

From the moment Hope and Faith were able to say, "Daddy", Robert preached to them the importance of having enough self-respect and courage to never tolerate a man physically or verbally abusing them. In fact, Melody could count on one hand the number of times that Robert had raised his voice in anger, let alone threatened her. So, she knew better than anyone that he'd try to burrow through the hardwood floor to get past her before he put his hands on her.

Melody's words were like kryptonite. Robert's scowl evaporated immediately. He walked backward until his legs bumped against the footboard of their king-sized bed and plopped down like a child who'd just been put in timeout.

Melody placed the tips of her fingers together and made a praying gesture, her hands positioned in front of her mouth as she walked toward her husband.

"Baby, I know you're upset, but I need you to calm down long enough to hear me out. People make mistakes. We all make mistakes. But people can change."

"Not an abuser," Robert mumbled.

"Let me finish, babe." Melody placed a hand on her hip and rubbed her forehead with the other while she searched

ANIMUS

for the right words. "I'm not asking you to forgive him for what he did to you and your mother. I'm just asking you to reconsider putting him out on the street."

"Reconsider! That man—"

"Is homeless," Melody interjected. "I know how much he hurt you, but I need you to follow your own advice right now. You are quick to tell me and the kids to never react to a situation, we should always respond. If you toss your dad out right now that is nothing but a reaction to your anger." Melody waved her hand around the bedroom. "Look at how God has blessed you despite how you grew up. You are a decorated veteran, college graduate, the owner of three businesses, we have a five-bedroom home, and beautiful kids. Enis may have hurt you, but God didn't let him break you."

Robert stared at his thighs and nodded in agreement.

"Which brings me to my next point. My sister is here with her kids and we still have enough room to let him stay. We can give Enis the guest room that Jalen is in. Jalen can move into the bedroom with his brothers. Hope and Faith are already in the same room."

"Those are teenage boys. They can't all sleep in the same bed."

"That's why God made blowup mattresses. Two of them can sleep in the bed and one can sleep on the blowup mattress."

Robert stood up and hugged Melody. He knew she meant well, but there was so much about his father that she didn't know. His hug was tight like a scared child hoping that the one adult he trusts wouldn't abandon him.

"He's an evil man, babe. It's my job to protect my family from people like him."

"Give him a chance, babe. This could be an opportunity for reconciliation. The kids need to know their grandfather. I would like to know my father-in-law. You can kick him out if he disrespects us, but at least wait to see how things work out." Melody took a step back and held Robert at

ANIMUS

arm's length. "Besides, how is it going to look if you let my sister and her kids stay but put your father out."

"I'm fine with that."

"I'm not because it ain't right. Must I remind you that the Lord giveth and He taketh away? Baby, all our blessings can be taken away from us in the blink of an eye. We could find ourselves homeless." Melody grabbed Robert's hand. "Honey, we are blessed so that we can be a blessing to others."

Robert pulled away and walked over to the bedroom window. He looked out at the backyard and watched the boys jump on the trampoline. Dealing with Enis was just one of his problems. He'd have to explain to Faith and Hope why he'd lied to them their entire life. He pressed upon them the importance of always telling the truth, but now he was guilty of the same moral crime he'd lectured them on.

"He can stay for a week."

"Babe, you know it's going to take more than a week for things to get worked out."

"Two weeks...then he's got to get the hell out of here."

Melody placed her hands on her hips and shook her head pathetically. She approached Robert from behind and hugged him.

"You're a good man, babe. I know you'll do the right thing." She patted Robert on the butt. "Now come on in here with me and let's face your dad. Let me do the talking...okay."

Robert nodded.

When they walked back into the living room, Enis was standing next to the fireplace staring at the framed pictures on the mantle.

"Where is EJ?" Melody asked.

"Oh, he left," Enis replied. "He said he had to go do a job somewhere. I think he said it was in Arlington, so he had to get going because it was far."

"Yeah, Arlington is about an hour away," Melody said. She looked back at Robert and grabbed his hand. "Robert and

ANIMUS

I have talked, and we would like you to stay for a few weeks until you can work out some arrangements."

"Thank you. I appreciate it."

"But there are some strings attached. One, you have to be actively looking for arrangements. The VA Hospital is on the other side of Dallas, at least an hour away, so if you need one of us to take you there to handle your business, we'll do that."

"I understand."

"Secondly, under no condition are you to be alone with the girls. No disrespect, but we don't know you. I don't let my girls be alone with men I don't know."

"Trust me, I understand that too. The only man they should be alone with is their father."

"Thank you," Melody said. "You'll be staying in one of the guest rooms. It has a bathroom, so you can get cleaned up in there. I'll get some of Rob's clothes for you to wear." Melody waved her hand in the direction of the kitchen. "Help yourself to whatever is in the refrigerator—we want you to feel comfortable."

"Melody, I really appreciate this," Enis said humbly. "I understand how complicated and scary this situation is for everyone. I won't disrespect your rules."

"Good. Well, I'm going to go out back and check on everyone." She looked at Robert with the same threatening stare she gave her girls whenever they were going to Walmart and she warned them to not ask for anything. "I *trust*, you guys will be okay in here."

Robert avoided eye contact.

"Right," Melody repeated and poked her husband in the belly with her index finger.

"Yeah," Robert mumbled and glared at Enis, "we good."

Melody feared that when she returned the place would be painted with Enis' blood. Nevertheless, she decided it was best to trust Robert to remain calm. After all, he was the most disciplined man she'd ever known. With his track record of self-control, she was able to be sanguine as she left the room.

Robert watched his lovely wife leave and then looked at the man he despised the most. A man who'd traumatized him so much during his childhood that he now suffered from post-traumatic stress disorder (PTSD).

"She's beautiful, son."

Robert moved closer. Enis took a step backward.

"Yeah, she is. Now let's cut the bullshit…why are you here? You lookin' for money?"

"Son, I'm just lookin' for shelter. I lost my house, car, furniture, clothes…everything. I never thought I'd be in this position. I've kept track of your success from long distance. You know me and your brother keep in touch, so he's always telling me how well y'all are doing out here. I never reached out to you because I knew you didn't want to talk to me…and I understand why. I…I just hope that we can come to a truce while I'm here."

Enis held out his hand to shake. Robert didn't bother to look at it.

"If it wasn't for Melody, I would've already tossed your ass outta here. You violate my house, my family, or me, in any way," Robert took another step closer, "and I'm going to put hands on you the way you put hands on my mother."

10

Enis locked the bedroom door and sat on the bed for a few minutes. He hadn't been face-to-face with Robert in nearly twenty years and although the encounter was potentially combustible, no blows were thrown. He'd cleared his first major hurdle—acceptance into Robert's house. Still, his mission had just begun. He'd need to tread carefully to accomplish his ultimate goal.

The guest bedroom was small, but tidier than any hotel room he'd ever stayed in. Matching bed, dresser, and nightstands. A ceiling fan that Enis figured cost more than his last car payment. Sheer drapes framed the large window that overlooked the backyard. And a 40" screen television was mounted on the wall.

Yeah, I could get used to this, Enis thought as he sized the place up.

ANIMUS

Enis looked at his cellphone and saw that he had three missed calls. He was not disappointed. The number belonged to Booker, the one man he wanted to avoid. Enis was so far on Booker's bad side that he pondered whether getting himself thrown in jail was safer than roaming the streets.

When Mother Nature woke up on the wrong side of the bed and decided to unleash her fury on the city of New Orleans, Enis wasn't as stressed as most residents. In fact, he saw it as an opportunity to flee his creditor and start anew. Apparently, Booker was also aware that Enis might use the natural disaster as an opportunity to vanish. The three phone calls within an hour span were proof of it.

"You can keep callin', but I ain't gon' answer," Enis mumbled.

No sooner than the words entered his tart mouth, bypassed his parched lips, and found freedom to roam, a text message came through—it was from Booker.

E, ain't a damn thing changed. You got until the 9th to come up with my 10K. I got people in Texas. Don't make me chase you.

Enis turned off the phone after reading the message. The hairs on his forearm stood up and a tingling sensation raced down his spine. He'd known Booker for thirty years and never knew the gap-toothed man to make a threat he didn't intend to carry out. Phase two of his plan would have to go into effect immediately.

A light rap of the door brought Enis back to the present moment.

"Hi, Enis, it's Melody."

Enis shoved the cellphone in his pocket and opened the door.

"Hey, I have some clothes here. A few t-shirts, pants, socks, and a pack of underwear that's never been opened. I always buy extra for Robert. I'm not sure if they'll fit, but—"

ANIMUS

"Don't worry, I'll make do." Enis smiled. "Even if I have to pin them up, they're better than what I have on."

"Right, right…oh, I also have here a travel kit. I stuffed it with a toothbrush, mouthwash, and other stuff that I thought you might need."

"Wow, are you always this efficient?"

Melody shrugged. "I had to go out and buy a bunch of those items when my sister came here with her boys. That's just some of the leftover stuff." She stammered like a woman ending a date with a man who was clearly waiting for a goodnight kiss. "Well, I'm going to let you get cleaned up. Let me know if you need anything else."

"I will."

Melody was about to turn and walk away, but Enis stopped her.

"Melody, wait." His voice was just above a whisper. "Robert would have thrown me out if you didn't speak up for me. I just want you to know that I appreciate that."

"Well, this is a stressful time for everyone. I just want us all to get through this with as little drama as possible. This will give y'all time to iron out your differences. I just want everyone to try and get along."

Melody took a few steps backward and then turned to walk away. She could feel Enis' eyes undressing her. When she glanced back and saw him in the doorway watching her a chill went down her spine. His eyes were piercing. His smirk—unnerving.

The hot shower water washed away a week's worth of funk. Enis decided to bask in the moment, standing under the steady stream like an outdoorsman who'd happened on an inviting waterfall. His thoughts clacked in his head to the point that they sounded like the big wheel on the Price is Right. Round and around they went until they landed on the most pleasant thought of all—Melody.

Enis squirted a large glob of shower gel into his hand and applied it to his hard penis. As he thought about his daughter-in-law in jeans that were so tight, he could see her camel toe, he stroked and groaned. Visualizing her getting undressed and unbuttoning her bra to allow those size C breasts—that Robert paid for—flop out and jiggle, was enough to provoke a more vigorous stroke and a deeper moan.

When his lust reached its zenith, Enis smacked the shower wall, aimed his penis downward, and unleashed more sperm than he knew his sixty-five-year-old body could produce. The spasm made his butt-cheeks flex and his knees buckle. He became light-headed and decided to slouch against the shower wall instead of dropping to one knee. A wall of steam swallowed his naked body as he slouched and panted like he'd just sprinted one hundred yards.

"Damn, I needed that," Enis mumbled.

He shook his head as if trying to free himself from masturbation's stranglehold. The hot water washed away the dirt from the storm as well as all evidence of his salacious act. Enis turned off the shower and allowed a wicked grin to emerge.

"Robert, you are one lucky son-of-a-bitch."

11

Darlene licked her fingers and chewed with her mouth open at the same time. She was an attractive woman but ate like a starved Neanderthal. She slurped the strawberry soda next to her plate and then belched in a way that most would consider unbecoming of a woman.

"And then what happened?" she asked.

EJ sat on the other end of the rickety dining table and used his fork to make tracks in his mashed potatoes. The clump of white mush looked like a chessboard. He spoke without looking up at his wife.

"Nothing much to tell. When Rob and Mel went into the bedroom to talk, I slipped out the front door."

"You just left your daddy there?"

"You don't see him here, do you?" EJ dropped the fork and grabbed his beer. He turned the beer up, staring at the water stain on the ceiling while he chugged, and then placed

ANIMUS

the bottle down on the table hard enough for it to make Darlene raise an eyebrow. "Rob looked like he wanted to kill me before Mel pulled him away. I got the hell out of there before they came back out. He's called me four times since I left. I ain't answerin'."

"You just gon' keep duckin' him?"

"I know my brother. He'll cool off in a few hours. I'll talk to him tomorrow."

"You hope. What did your daddy say before you left?"

"Nothing. He's the one who told me to leave."

"That's ballsy. How did he know they were going to let him stay?"

"I don't know. I guess he figured if Rob was going to throw him out, he would've already done it." EJ shrugged. "He ain't called me yet, so I guess everything is okay."

"What I can't understand is why Rob hates your daddy so much. You grew up in the same house and you seem to get along good with the man. What did he do to Rob to make him lie about the man being alive?"

EJ finished off his beer and tossed the bottle in the garbage can a few feet away. "I don't know what the hell is wrong with Rob. He says my pops was abusive."

"Was he?"

"Not to me. Honestly, I don't remember him beating on my mama the way Rob says he did. My mama died when I was thirteen, Rob was around eighteen. He says I was too young to remember the stuff that went down. I mean...I saw him smack Rob a few times, but it wasn't no more than any other kid in the 'hood gets hit. We used to be bad as hell. Half those licks we earned."

"Did he smack you?"

"Not that I can recall."

"So, how you gon' say *we*? You obviously didn't have the same experience with your daddy that Rob had. Did he like you more than he liked Rob?"

"That's a stupid question."

ANIMUS

"No, it's not. Every parent likes one kid more than the others. They may not admit it, but they do. I know my mama liked my sister more than she liked me. She used to treat me like shit because I was darker than my sister. My grandmother treated my sister better too. When my sister got hit by that car and died, they never stopped mourning. When the police couldn't find the hit and run driver, my mama and grandmother took their frustration out on me."

"Well, I don't think it's about whether he likes me more than Rob."

"What do you think it is?"

"I don't know, but it ain't got shit to do with me."

"So, let me make sure I got this right…you know they don't get along, but you still brought your daddy over there? You could've at least waited until you got the down payment money from Rob before you pissed him off."

"You sure you wanna go there again? I told you I'm working on something."

Darlene rolled her eyes and dowsed the piece of chicken she held with Crystal hot sauce.

"That's your third piece of chicken. Why are you so hungry?"

Darlene stopped as if she'd been zapped with a stun gun. She put the hot sauce bottle down and wiped her hands.

"Umm, I didn't wanna bring this up."

"Bring what up?"

"Umm…I'm pregnant."

"You got jokes."

"Do I look or sound like I'm joking?"

EJ studied Darlene's facial expression for a second and realized she wasn't joking. Now he was the one who looked like he'd been zapped with the stun gun. He stood up and with two long strides was at the refrigerator sifting through the leftovers and spoiled milk to get to the last beer. He ripped off the bottle cap and chugged so hard that his Adam's apple danced in his throat.

ANIMUS

"Damn, it's like that?" Darlene's rhetorical question lacked the flippancy her words normally carried. She seemed hurt by his response. "I tell you I'm pregnant and you need to get another beer."

"How far gone are you?"

"Too far to get an abortion so don't even ask?"

"I didn't say I wanted you—"

"You didn't have to say it. It's written all over your face." She carried her chicken over to the garbage can and dumped the plate. "For the record, I'm three months pregnant. I've been waiting for the right time to tell you." She turned and walked away. Without looking back, she said, "I hope you're ready to be a daddy."

EJ waited until he heard the bedroom door close before he let out the word that begged to be set free. "Fuck!"

The thought of one day being a father was intriguing, but his bank account would only allow it to be fleeting. They'd talked about having a child but agreed that buying a house should come first. Darlene assured him that the necessary precautions were being taken to prevent an unplanned pregnancy. Now he had the pressure of proving for a child to go along with his mounting debt. His thoughts were all over the place.

She was supposed to be taking that shot to keep from getting pregnant. She must've forgot to take it or missed an appointment or something. The bottom line is, she was supposed to make sure she didn't get pregnant. He tossed the remote on the sofa, collapsed the footrest, and leaped off the chair. *If she thinks she's just gonna drop this news on me and walk away, she dun' bumped her damn head. She gon' explain this shit to me.*

Before he could make it to the hallway that led to their bedroom, there was a heavy knock at the front door.

"Who is this knocking on my door like the damn police?" He pivoted in the direction of the door and then stopped. "Shit, what if it is the police?"

ANIMUS

EJ rushed over to the coffee table and grabbed the ashtray with the half-smoked blunt in it. He put the ashtray under the sofa and sprayed Lysol until the room was cloudy. Satisfied that anything incriminating was hidden, he headed over to the front door and opened it.

Robert stormed in gestapo-style. He gripped EJ's collar and shoved him backward.

"What the fuck were you thinking, bringing that man to my house?"

EJ wrangled free of his brother's stronghold. "I already explained to you that he couldn't come here. Besides, you got more than enough room at your house."

"You know I don't fuck with Enis! You should've called me!"

"You right. I should've called first. I guess I was just thinking—"

"You were thinking it's easier to ask for forgiveness than it is to get permission."

"Rob, you and I both know you would've said *no* if I'd called you first."

"You're damn right I would've."

"That's why I didn't call you." Enis pointed at the sofa. "You gon' beat my ass or have a seat."

Robert reluctantly sat down.

"Y'all okay in here?"

"Yeah, baby, we're good."

"Hey, Dee. We're good. I'm sorry if I startled you. I just had to check my lil brother."

"He probably deserved it," Darlene joked and smiled. "You want something to drink?"

"No, thank you."

EJ noticed how many teeth his wife was suddenly showing. Whenever Robert came around, Darlene turned into Susie Sunshine. On more than one occasion he'd brought his observation to her attention, but it didn't stop her from batting

ANIMUS

her eyelashes and walking with a more pronounced twist when Robert came over.

"I said, we're good. You can go back in the room now. We need to talk."

"Did you tell him the news yet?"

EJ pointed at the bedroom. Darlene rolled her eyes, spun on her heels, and vanished down the hallway.

"What news?"

EJ walked over and sat on the recliner. He pulled the lever and the leg rest popped up.

"She's pregnant."

"Dude, are you ready for that kind of responsibility?" EJ waved his hand at his not-so-flattering home. "Do I look like I'm ready?"

"Right now, I've got my own problems." Robert sighed. "Look, Enis has two weeks to get his shit together and then you need to come and get him."

"What does Melody have to say about it."

"You know her, she'd take in a stray cat if it wandered up to our door. I'm quarterbacking this one." Robert held up two fingers. "Two weeks. Then you need to come and get him."

"And take him where?"

"You can take his ass to hell for all I care."

Robert left without saying goodbye. When the front door closed, EJ retrieved the ashtray he'd stashed under the sofa and lit the blunt. After taking a puff he mumbled, "Nah playa, you gon' have to pay me to come and get him."

12

Enis appeared from the shadows of the hallway with measured steps. He looked like a nervous singer stepping on stage at the Apollo Theatre during Amateur Night. Melody and Kim sipped wine and watched him from their barstool perches.

"Feel better?" Melody asked.

"Much better," Enis said.

"Oh, this is my sister, Kim. Kim this is Enis...Robert's father."

"Nice to meet you." Enis stuck out his hand to shake. Kim gripped the tip of his wrinkled fingers and gave a half-hearted shake. "You two look like twins."

"She wishes," Kim teased.

"You want something to drink?" Melody asked and held up the wine bottle.

ANIMUS

"I gave up alcohol years ago, but I could use some coffee."

"I'll get a pot brewing."

"Thanks."

"Where do you live?" Kim asked.

"In a little scatter-sight in the 9th ward. Right off Claiborne. What about you?"

"I own a little house Uptown in the 17th."

"Gert Town?"

"Hollygrove."

"Oh okay. Well, hopefully y'all didn't get too much flooding around there."

"Unfortunately, we did. It floods around my house when there is a regular thunderstorm. When that water from Katrina got higher than my porch and started coming in my front door, I grabbed my kids and left."

"Good thinking."

"I noticed you were limping," Melody said. "How'd you hurt your leg?"

"I slipped and sliced my leg on a piece of metal while helping an old lady in my building get to the roof." Enis lied and rubbed his thigh. "She's eighty years old, but I managed to get her up there. That flood water can make an old man like me find a way."

"Oh my. Do you need to go to the doctor?"

"Already did. It hurt like hell at first, but once they rescued me and got me to the VA, the doctors patched me up and gave me some strong ibuprofen. I'll be alright. I suffered worse than this during the war."

"Well, at least you made it out," Melody said. "A lot of people didn't."

"You're right about that daughter-in-law. I watched a body float past me like a log."

"Yeah, we saw one in the Superdome."

The backdoor opened and Faith came running in. Hope was hot on her heels.

ANIMUS

"What are y'all doing?" Melody shouted.

"We want some water," Faith said.

"Y'all need to get *in* some water," Kim said. "Y'all smell like two puppies."

"Aww they are fine. Even if they do smell like outside, my babies are still little cuties." Enis opened his arms. "Can I get a hug?"

The girls both looked at Melody to see if it was okay. Melody gave the green light with a slight head nod.

"Are you really our granddaddy?" Hope asked. "Daddy told us our granddaddy died in a war?"

"It's called the Vietnam War, stupid," Faith said.

"You're stupid." Hope fired back and shoved Faith hard enough to make her stagger.

"Cut it out," Kim ordered.

"Yes, I was in the Vietnam War, but as y'all can see…I'm not dead."

"So, why did daddy say you were dead?" Faith asked.

"That's enough questions," Melody said. "Kim, would you mind taking them in the bathroom and making sure they get cleaned up."

"I don't mind at all," Kim said. "Come on you two. Y'all smell worse than your cousins."

Kim led the girls out of the kitchen. Enis sat down on a stool.

"How do you like your coffee?"

"Black…no sugar, no cream."

Melody brought over a cup of steaming coffee.

"Thank you." Enis took a sip. "Taste like home."

"It is. The Tom Thumb up the street sells Café Du Monde coffee and Community coffee. I stock up on both of 'em."

"Y'all really doing good for yourselves. Business must be good."

"Yes, all of the businesses are doing good. But you know that already."

ANIMUS

"Yeah, I can't lie, I've been keeping track of y'all progress. Rob has my work ethic."

"So, you're taking credit for my work ethic now?" Robert said.

"Oh, babe, I didn't hear you come in."

"Yeah, I came in just in time to hear ole Enis here say I take after him."

Melody hurried over to Robert and kissed him. She made sure to position herself between father and son.

"Are you hungry? I was just about to order some chicken from Popeyes." She looked at Enis. "Do you like Popeyes chicken?"

"I'll just eat some of their red beans and rice and a biscuit. I can't eat anything too tough. Every time I try to bite into something tough, I'm afraid the few teeth I have left will get stuck in it. I'll be walking around here with nothing but my gums showing in the front of my mouth."

"I can think of a few other ways to remove the teeth from your mouth," Robert growled and cracked his knuckles.

Melody was so uncomfortable that she wanted to run out of the house. Never had she been exposed to this level of vitriol. The gloom of the moment left her at a loss for words. So, she did the only thing that she could, she whispered, "It's gon' be alright, baby."

"Yeaaaah, it's gon' be alright," Robert said, the words oozed from his mouth while his eyes remained glued on Enis.

To say things were tense at that moment would be an understatement. In fact, bloodshed was a possibility if it hadn't been for the boys entering the house.

"Tee Melody. What's for dinner?" Jalen asked.

"Y'all have perfect timing," Melody said with all sincerity. "I'm ordering some chicken. Y'all go get cleaned up. Honey, why don't you go get cleaned up too."

It took a slight shove from Melody to get Robert to move, but he did.

"Thanks," Enis said.

ANIMUS

"Don't thank me yet. I can't promise I'm going to be here to run interference the next time."

Robert chose to eat dinner in his office. Afterwards, he and Melody retreated to the bedroom earlier than they had in months. Robert stared up at the ceiling while Melody laid next to him with her head on his chest.

"Babe, how long are you gonna act like this? Why don't you just try to talk to him?"

"I ain't got shit to say to that man."

"I don't get it. I mean, I know some bad stuff went down, but I still feel lost about what transpired between y'all. I mean, all you've ever told me about your dad is that he was abusive to your mom and you. That's all you've ever said."

"What more do I need to say? He was abusive to us. And by *us*, I mean me and my mother. I don't think he ever as much as raised his voice to EJ."

"I guess I'm just trying to understand what that looks like. I mean, EJ seems to love your dad. Hell, he's got his name tattooed on his forearm."

"EJ didn't have the same experience as me, Melody!"

"Why are you raising your voice? I'm just trying to understand. I mean, we grew up in the 'hood. I used to see my uncles whoop their sons. The beatings they used to give those boys would probably be considered child abuse today, but they were commonplace back then. I'm just asking for clarity, so I can have a better understanding of what you went through. The girls really like your dad and they just met him. And I've gotta be honest, he's been nice to me too." *Despite the creepy way he looked at me,* Melody thought before continuing. "I just don't see the man that you've described."

Robert sighed and ran his hand across his face and flapped his lips in exasperation the way kids do when they make the motorbike sound.

ANIMUS

"The man you've met is not the man that raised me. The man that raised me was as mean as a water moccasin." Robert sighed. "Honestly, when I see him, it reminds me of how complicit I was in his abuse. Not the physical, but the emotional abuse."

"What do you mean?"

"I used to help him cheat."

Melody propped up on her elbows. "What?"

"It started when I was in high school; around the tenth grade. Enis used to have women call the house and ask to speak to me. When I got on the phone, they'd ask me where he was. I'd wait a few seconds and then give him a signal. He'd go into another room when my mom wasn't around and pick up the other phone. Then I'd hang up and let him talk. That shit used to happen two or three times a week."

"Why'd you do it?"

"Because he told me if I didn't, he'd have to take his frustration out on my mama. I knew what that meant."

"He was going to beat her."

"Yeah. And I knew he meant it. This is the same man who beat my mother up in the middle of the street in front of all my classmates when I was in elementary school."

Melody rubbed Robert's arm as a show of affection. It was all she could do to allay a wound that was obviously too deep for her to reach.

"I remember one night, I must've been fifteen or sixteen, I was sitting in the living room watching TV. They'd just bought a house out in the east. Life seemed to be looking up for our family. You know back in the eighties, if you bought a house in the east black folk in New Orleans thought you were rich."

Melody nodded in agreement.

"Anyway, I was watching TV and he walked up to me and whispered in my ear. You'll never believe what that man asked me."

"What?"

ANIMUS

"He asked me if I had an extra condom."

"What!"

"Yep...he asked me, his teenage son, if I had an extra condom that he could use to go fuck some other woman."

"What did you say?"

"I told him where I kept them." Tears bubbled in Robert's eyes. "When he left that night, I went to my room and buried my face in my pillow. A few hours later, I heard my mother in her bedroom crying. I don't know why she was crying, but I figured it was because she knew her husband was out doing dirt. What she didn't know was that I helped him." Robert rubbed the frown lines on his forehead. "You have no idea how hard it was for me to look my mother in the face sometimes. I wanted to tell her everything I knew about him, but I also wanted to protect her—emotionally and physically. I was afraid that if I told her, she'd confront him and then he'd beat the shit out of her and that would've ended up being my fault too. So, I just kept all the shit I knew about him to myself."

"Wow. That's a terrible position to put a child in."

"You never hear me using the word *hate* because I'm not sure I know what hate feels like, but if there is a such thing as hate, that's what I have in my heart for that man."

Melody caressed Robert's face. He was the strongest man she'd ever known. But at that moment, with the covers pulled up close to his neck, he looked like a child attempting to hide from the Boogie Man.

"Baby, I'm not sure what hate looks or feels like either, but I know that we're all predisposed to love our parents. Deep down, I'm sure you still love your dad; you just don't like him."

Robert took a moment to ponder Melody's remark and then craned his neck to kiss her.

"I don't know if what I feel is hatred or a strong dislike, but what I do know is that I don't want him around my family."

"Umm, I did something that I know you're not going to be very happy about."

ANIMUS

"What?"

"I contacted Dr. Miles."

"Why?"

"Because I think it's time you spoke to him again. You've still been having dreams about killing your father and now the father that you pretended was dead is here in the flesh. I think you need to talk to Dr. Miles about this."

"Mel, you know I don't like talking to a damn shrink."

"He's a highly respected psychiatrist."

"He's a shrink who charges $200 an hour. All he did the two times I went to see him was sit there with his legs crossed and nod every few minutes. He kept asking me questions but didn't offer any answers. Total waste of my time. I could've gotten better advice from a wino in the 'hood and it wouldn't have cost me nothin' but a pint of whiskey."

"It's not a waste of time, baby. He can help you talk through your problems. Black folk—especially black men—have got to get over the stigma of getting help."

"Mel, don't come at me with that "black men are too prideful to see a therapist" crap. I'm a black man in America. On top of that, I belong to the group of black men who've been treated the worst since we were brought to this country—the dark-skinned black man.

"When the slave master needed more slaves, he made the big black bucks do the breeding. We even had to stand there and watch our women be raped. And when the white women on the plantation stared at us a little too hard, the slave master had no problem castrating us. If we refused to submit and fought back, we were broken. Have you ever heard of Buck Breaking?"

"No," Melody said.

"I'll spare you the details, but just know, it's the most emasculating thing that can be done to a man."

"What's your point, baby?"

"My point is, despite all the bullshit black men—particularly dark-skinned black men—have gone through since

ANIMUS

we were brought to this country, none of those black men needed to see a damn shrink to survive. We didn't need to *express our feelings* so that we can feel better back then, and I don't believe we need it in present times. We dealt with the shit that was thrown at us. We became masters at turning chicken shit into chicken salad...and we're still doing that to this day."

"Times have changed, baby."

"No, they haven't. We've changed. All this needing to see a shrink crap is just another thing white folk do that black folk have adopted to assimilate. We used to keep our dogs in the yard, now you see black folk riding in our cars with dogs on our laps—white folk shit. We used to spank our kids when they were disrespectful, now we're doing ass backwards stuff like putting them in timeout—white folk shit. And we used to figure out ways to deal with our problems, now we're paying people $200 an hour to listen to us vent—more white folk shit."

When Robert finished his soliloquy, he could almost hear his heart thumping. His throat was dry, and he felt lightheaded. He noticed Melody staring aimlessly at the wall adjacent their bed.

"Mel, I know you mean well, but I—"

"Dr. Miles said he could fit you in tomorrow morning at ten. I went ahead and scheduled your visit. You can go if you want to." Melody didn't expect to be hit with a verbal barrage like that. Since she didn't have a comeback laced with equal passion, she quietly turned over and pulled the covers up to her neck. "Good night."

13

September 5, 2005/McKinney, TX. 7:27 a.m.

The city of New Orleans may have been going through the worst natural disaster in U.S. history, but the rest of the country functioned as usual. Monday morning came as scheduled and the fireball in the sky was in all its glory. When Melody made it to the kitchen, Kim was already sitting on a stool reading the newspaper.

"Good morning," Kim said.

"Good morning. You're up early."

"I told you I was going to be ready to go stand in that Red Cross line to see what they are offering. I plan on getting the free food stamps the government is giving out too."

ANIMUS

"Did you sleep good?"

"Like a baby. That's why I'm wide awake now. I slipped out and went to bed right after y'all went in the bedroom."

"I'm sorry I had to leave you in here last night. My husband was on ten. I had to give him some to calm his nerves. Let me go round up these girls for school and we can leave."

"I already took care of that. It wasn't easy getting them up. All five of them were in here laughing and playing Monopoly when I went to bed. No tellin' how long they stayed up. I had to turn on that bedroom light and beat on the dresser to wake 'em up, but they finally opened those pretty eyes. I brought them some cereal. They should be dressed by now."

"Thank you, Sis." Melody hugged Kim from behind. "We can swing by Starbucks after I drop the girls off at school."

"Cool. You think I should wake up the boys and make them come with us?"

"Let those kids sleep. I know they don't feel like standing in a line all morning."

"True. I know Josh will probably start complaining after ten minutes."

"We're ready," Faith shouted as she entered the living room.

Hope didn't appear as enthusiastic. She wore a frown like someone had belched in her face.

"I can see which is the morning child and which one isn't," Kim said.

"Girl, they are like night and day," Melody said. "Come on y'all, let's go. Me and Tee Kim have a lot to do today."

The engine under the hood of the SUV growled when Melody turned the key. She eased out of the garage and they were on their way. Less than five minutes into the drive, Faith and Hope were engaged in their routine bickering.

"You kept the lick," Faith said and tapped Hope's arm.

"You kept it," Hope said and tapped Faith's arm.

ANIMUS

Faith hit Hope again. "You kept it."

Hope returned the pat. "You kept it."

"Do they fight like this all the time?" Kim asked.

"All day, every day. But let someone else mess with them. Hope will cut you to the white meat if you mess with Faith and vice versa. Robert and I had to go to a conference last year because they jumped on a little white boy who was bullying Faith." Melody glanced at her twins through the rearview mirror. "Y'all cut it out back there!"

"Yeah, I remember you tellin' me about that. I'll bet he didn't mess with her again."

"Girl, when we were in the principal's office, you could cut the tension with a knife."

"Let me guess, they tried to make the little boy the victim."

"You know they did, but we weren't having it. By the time we arrived, I had a list of names of students who witnessed the bullying and permission from their parents to call their child in to testify if need be."

"They weren't ready for that."

"Hell no. And they especially weren't ready for Robert." Melody chuckled. "Girl, he looked that little snout-nosed boy's dad in the face and told that man, 'The next time your son hits one of my girls, I'm gon' hit you'."

"Yes indeed!" Kim laughed and clapped her hands. "I wish I could've been there to see that. Girl what did you do?"

"At first I got nervous…I thought Rob was about to jump across the table and beat the man up." A sly grin appeared on Melody's face. She looked at Kim and said, "Then I got hot."

"Baaaaby, I know that's right."

The sisters gave each other a high-five.

"Are y'all ready for school today?" asked Kim.

"Yeah!" Faith said.

"No!" Hope said.

"Hope, why aren't you ready for school?" Kim asked.

ANIMUS

"I'm tired of school."

"I know why she's tired of school," Melody said. "Those fractions are kicking her butt."

"What kind of fractions?"

"Improper fractions."

"Girl, I hated fractions."

"Me too. I be struggling trying to help them with their homework." Melody looked in her rearview mirror. "Y'all tell your teacher that we tried to work on your fraction homework, but we didn't understand some of it. Show her the problems we couldn't figure out and ask her to explain them."

"We don't need to do that," Faith said.

"Why not?" Melody asked.

"Because Grandpa Enis helped us do them."

"When?"

"Last night!" the twins said in unison.

"You and Daddy went to sleep," Hope said. "After we finished playing Monopoly, we started doin' our homework at the kitchen table. Jalen tried to help but he didn't know nothing. So, Grandpa Enis came in the kitchen and helped us."

"He was doing it easy too, Mama," Faith said.

Kim turned up the volume on the radio and asked, "Well…how do you feel about him helping them with their homework?"

"Honestly, I don't know how I feel about it. Robert always said he was the smartest man he's ever known. He used to be an accountant."

"Really?"

"Yeah. Robert told me he used to do the books for a lot of nightclubs in New Orleans. You know…making the numbers look the way they want 'em to look to get around the I.R.S. Robert told me that when he was child, Enis used to sit around and do calculus problems when he was bored."

"Damn, it's like that. Hell, if he's that good, he can help my boys with math."

ANIMUS

"I'm sure he will. Especially, if it'll get him closer to helping their mama with a thing or two. I saw him peeking at that big ole booty."

"Girl please," Kim said and sucked her teeth. "He's a handsome old man, but I can't mess with nobody who is old enough to be my daddy." Kim held up a finger. "Unless he's rich."

"Slut."

"Sometimes," Kim replied with a mischievous grin.

"Is he really our grandpa?" Faith asked.

"He told us to call him Grandpa Enis," Hope added. "Mama, are we supposed to call him grandpa?"

"Umm, we can talk about that later. And as far as him helping y'all with that homework, let's keep that between us. I don't want your daddy to know."

"Why not?" Faith asked.

"Umm, because…" Melody stuttered and scratched her forehead again.

"Because your daddy was just telling me how smart y'all are," Kim blurted. "He might not like it if he found out Enis helped y'all with your homework. That's gon' make him think y'all can't do it yourself. Do y'all want your dad to think y'all can't do your homework?"

"No!" the girls answered in harmony.

"Well, y'all should probably avoid mentioning that to your daddy."

Melody mouthed: *Thank you.*

Kim winked.

Melody turned into the school's drop off lane and stopped in front of the entrance. "Alright, girls. Y'all have a good day, and I want y'all standing out here when I come to get you. Don't make me have to come looking for y'all."

The girls shouted their goodbyes and leapt out of the car. Melody and Kim watched them skip into the school.

"I'll bet you need that coffee now, huh?" Kim said.

ANIMUS

"Coffee my ass," Melody replied and pressed the gas. "I feel like I need a martini."

Robert walked into the office building that he owned which housed all three of his companies. Per his normal routine, he made the rounds to each company with a cup of coffee in one hand and an intense look on his face.

"Good morning, Mr. Rob," said Lucy, the receptionist at RTS Pool Cleaning. She handed Rob a clipboard that showed the day's schedule. "We've got three jobs this morning. The guys are out back packing up their gear."

"Thanks, Lucy. How was your weekend?"

"Fine. I started out trying to relax with a good book, but I got sucked into all the coverage about Hurricane Katrina. Damn shame how all those levies broke in mostly the black neighborhoods. How is your family?"

"Everybody is doing fine. Thanks for asking."

"That's good. Let me know if I can do anything to help."

"I appreciate that. We're good for now, but I've got a house full of teenage boys, plus Hope and Faith. You can babysit if you want."

"Anything but babysit." Lucy laughed. "There is a reason why I don't have kids. I like my peace and quiet. But if you need anything else, I'm your woman."

Robert smiled and handed the clipboard back to Lucy. He left the pool company and walked down the hall to RTS Janitorial. Jean Michele—JM was his nickname—was the receptionist at that company. A flamboyant gay man with a gift for gab and a proclivity for overreacting.

"Mr. Rob!" Jean Michele shouted and moved from behind his desk with his arms spread wide. "I've gotta give you a hug this morning because I know you need it. I've been glued to the news all weekend. I can't believe all the damage that hurricane caused to your hometown. Is your family safe?"

Rob gave Jean Michele a church hug. Not that he wanted to, but he didn't have much of a choice. Jean Michele was a touchy-feely kind of guy. Innocent. Sincere. But annoying at times. Rob tolerated his "extra" behavior because the man was his most reliable employee. He'd never missed a day of work in four years, and he was a customer service wiz.

"I appreciate it, JM. My entire family is safe. Thanks for asking. What we got this morning?"

"Same stuff, different day. All invoices paid and no complaints. That's all I worry about—those invoices and complaints."

"You and me both," Rob said. "I'm gon' get out of your hair. You know how to reach me if you need me."

Rob scooted out of the office before JM peppered him with personal questions that he didn't feel like answering. RTS Landscaping was located at the end of the long hallway. His entrepreneurial baby. It was the first company he opened, had the most employees, and was still the most profitable of all his business ventures. It was no surprise to anyone that it was the company he spent the most time overseeing.

When Rob walked into the office, the first person he saw was EJ standing in front of a large map of the city with push pins in it that represented the various subdivisions they'd been hired to maintain.

"Hey, big bro, I didn't know you were here. I didn't see your car in the parking lot."

"Mel's driving the Escalade. I'm in her car."

"I was just about to head out to Fossil Creek."

"You need to head to my house and get Enis."

"What happened?"

"He needs to get his ass over to the Red Cross and get whatever assistance they are offering so he can hurry up and get the hell out of my house."

"I have to go to Fossil Creek. That's our new account."

Animus

"I'll go over there and make sure everything is going smoothly. You need to go make sure Enis is straight. You brought him to my house; he's your responsibility."

EJ finished the coffee he was drinking, crushed the Styrofoam cup, and tossed it into the waste basket. "How long do I have to do this?"

"Until he gets what he needs and get the hell out of my house. You can take off for the rest of the week to taxi him around for all I care. I want him gone." Rob pointed at the door. "See ya'."

⁂

Enis peered into the garage and saw Melody's Audi and Robert's SUV gone. Only Melody's old Lexus was parked.

Looks like everybody's gone. I can finally check this place out.

Moving as stealthily as a burglar, he went upstairs to the bedroom where the boys slept and opened the door wide enough to peer in. They were all sound asleep. Enis closed the door without making a sound and strolled back downstairs.

The first stop on his inspection was the refrigerator, where he grabbed a few grapes with his unwashed hands and chased them with a swig of orange juice straight from the bottle. The next stop was the living room. He touched and examined everything in sight.

After going into the guest bedroom where Kim slept, Enis sifted through the dresser drawers, paying special attention to her panties, before making his way back to the living room.

Yeah, you doin' real good, Rob. A couple of these paintings could probably pay off my debt to Booker. I'll bet you got a safe in here somewhere too. Where would you keep your safe? Enis stood in the middle of the living room and scratched his unshaven face. He snapped his fingers. *Your office.*

Enis entered Robert's office cautiously, scanning the floor as if he expected it to be booby trapped. When he was

ANIMUS

confident there were no tripwires, he walked around, moving pictures on the wall until he found the one that had a safe behind it.

"Bingo," he muttered.

The safe had a dial on it, so Enis immediately started searching the desk drawers hoping to find a combination scribbled on a piece of paper. He shuffled through a few papers but came up empty.

At least I know where the safe is. I just gotta keep my ears open for clues on what the combination might be.

Enis made sure everything was in the same order in which he found it and then he closed the desk drawer. Satisfied that the picture which kept the safe hidden showed no signs of having been touched, he tip-toed out of the office and closed the door quietly behind him.

"Who are you?"

Enis jumped and grabbed his heart like Fred Sanford.

"Shit...you scared me!"

"Who are you?"

"I'm Enis Sumina. Robert's daddy. Who are you?"

"My name is Gloria, and I'm going to call Mr. Rob."

"I'm Robert's dad."

"Mr. Rob's papa is dead. Estás mintiendo."

"Huh. What does that mean?"

"It means...you're lying! And if I can't get in touch with Mr. Rob, I'm calling the police."

The short, long-haired woman did a military style about-face and mumbled something in Spanish as she mached toward the kitchen. Enis couldn't understand what she was saying, but he could tell by her body language and tone that it wasn't good.

"Wait, wait," Enis said and grabbed Gloria's arm, "let me explain."

"Don't touch me!" Gloria raised her fist. "You don't touch me!"

Animus

"I'm sorry! I'm sorry!" Enis held up his hands as if he were being robbed. "Miss, I didn't mean to touch you or scare you. I'm not going to hurt you, I swear. Like I said, my name is Enis Sumina. I'm, Mr. Rob's...daaaaaad."

"Why do you talk like that? My English isn't perfect, but good enough to understand you." She stepped toward Enis and asked sarcastically, "Okaaay, Mr. Rob's daaaaad. Why are you in his office? Only Mrs. Mel and me, go in his office."

Enis was saved by the doorbell. Gloria pointed a stiff wrinkled index finger at Enis. "You wait right here."

She walked over and opened the front door.

"Hey, Ms. Gloria."

Gloria grabbed EJ's arm and drug him in the house. She didn't utter a word until they were in the hallway that led to Rob's office.

"Mr. EJ, is this your papa?"

EJ chuckled. "Yeah."

"Mr. Rob told me his papa was dead."

"It's a long story Ms. Gloria, but trust me, this is our dad."

Gloria looked Enis up and down and aimed that wrinkled finger at him again. "You stay out of that office."

"Okay...damn."

Gloria marched off mumbling more words in Spanish.

"What the hell is wrong with her?" Enis asked.

"No, what the hell is wrong with you?" EJ replied. "Why were you in Rob's office? I don't even go in there."

"I was just checkin' it out."

"If you know what's best for you, you'd stay away from that office. Rob is already looking for a reason to kick you out. You'd better hope she don't tell him she caught you in there."

"I ain't thinkin' 'bout that old heifer," Enis said and waved dismissively. "Why are you here this time of morning?"

"To get you."

"Why?"

ANIMUS

"Because Rob told me to. He expects me to taxi you around the city so you can get whatever kind of public assistance you can get. He wants you out of here ASAP. Go get dressed. I'm gon' grab something to munch on in the kitchen."

"See if you can calm that old hag down."

"I'll deal with her; you just get dressed."

14

The Miles Counseling Center was in a two-story building in Frisco, Texas, that housed several doctor's offices. The carpeted hallway was flanked by towering mahogany doors labeled with gold rectangular plaques engraved with the names of the practitioners. The last time Robert visited Dr. Miles' office it was in a building in South Dallas with dingy carpet and located two blocks away from a liquor store where groups of men stood outside drinking Boone's Farm, Wild Irish Rose, and other types of cheap liquor while shooting dice. Arguments and fist fights were commonplace and there was enough gunplay to make standing outside a risky endeavor.

The doctor must've got more suckers to pay his two hundred dollar an hour fee. This place is a come up, Robert thought as he strolled down the hallway looking for the gold plaque with Dr. Miles' name on it.

ANIMUS

When he spotted his destination, Robert went inside—glancing back to make sure no one he recognized was watching. He was immediately impressed by the classy artwork that adorned the walls. The floors were shiny enough to eat off and the furniture looked as if it had just been delivered from the store. The only thing that wasn't impressive was the receptionist. Her tone was flat, eye contact non-existent, and the robotic way she greeted Robert when he walked in suggested she didn't want to be there.

An entrepreneur to his core, who understood the importance of good customer service, it took every bit of restraint he could summon to keep from challenging the woman's attitude. It was a good thing he found the restraint because the way she chewed and popped her gum, glanced at her cellphone every few seconds, examined her too long fake nails, and fiddled with weave that was longer than a horses' tail, suggested there was a high probability she wouldn't be receptive to constructive criticism. In fact, she looked like she kept guys named, Bookie and Ray-Ray, on speed dial should she need goon support.

Robert filled out the requisite forms and sat down. A woman who appeared to be in her forties sat next to a teenage boy a few chairs over. The woman whispered in the boy's ear while he sat with his arms crossed, appearing to be disinterested in what she had to say. Robert's paternal instincts were going haywire. He wanted to snatch the kid up by the collar to make him stop slouching and show his mother some respect. Once again, he needed to show restraint. Getting involved in other folks parenting struggles was a road he'd traveled before and regretted ever since.

Once, while traveling on an airplane from Miami to Dallas, a kid that couldn't have been more than seven years old was being a brat in the seat across the aisle from him. The mother appeared so flustered by the boy's refusal to listen that Robert felt compelled to intervene. He craned his neck to make eye contact with the child and shot a mean-mug that made the

105

chubby terror sit down and not utter another sound for the remainder of the flight.

When the deboarding process started, the mother and child got off first. As Robert approached the exit, the flight attendant pulled him to the side and handed him a note. It was from the brat's mother. The note read:

I don't appreciate you intimidating my boy. If I wanted your help, I would have asked for it.

Robert made a vow to himself to never stick his nose into someone else's parenting business again, but being the disciplinarian that he was, the urge to intervene jabbed at him like hunger pains while he waited in the lobby for his name to be called.

To keep his mind off going "daddy" on a child that wasn't his, he decided to focus on the coffee table littered with magazines. Black Enterprise, Sports Illustrated, Cosmopolitan, and an assortment of other publications were placed there with the intention of distracting clients who might otherwise opt to leave. Robert thumbed through a three-month-old Sports Illustrated magazine and wondered if he should walk out and lie to Melody if she asked if he went.

Fifteen minutes later, the door located to the right of the receptionist desk swung open and a slender, gray-haired man wearing wire frame glasses stuck half of his body out.

"Mr. Sumina. Please, come in."

Damn. Why he gotta say my name all loud, Robert thought, feeling self-conscious about his identity being revealed.

He dropped the magazine and followed the man into the long hallway.

"It's good to see you again. I was surprised when your wife contacted me, but I'm glad you're back. How have you been?"

"So-so," Robert said lazily. "Hey, I know it's none of my business, but your receptionist is kind of—"

ANIMUS

"Rude and unprofessional...I know. Trust me, I would have fired her a long time ago, but she's my sister-in-law. If I let her go, my wife would make me sleep outside."

"Understood," Robert replied.

They walked into the doctor's spacious office. The wall behind his desk was wall-papered with degrees and certificates. The shelf to the left was cluttered with framed pictures of the doctor with celebrities such as: Tiger Woods, Michael Jordan, Charles Barkley, and others. Robert didn't recall seeing the pictures the last time he visited.

"Big sports fan, huh?" Robert said and pointed at the pictures.

"I used to be. Nothing more than a casual fan these days. Too busy to attend many events."

"That's a good problem to have."

"If you say so. Most of those pictures were taken in the late 90's when I was heavy into sports psychology."

"Wow. Were all those stars your clients?"

"Some. But if I told you which ones were my clients, I'd have to kill you." The corners of the doctor's lips curled upward. "That information is confidential." Dr. Miles held up his finger. "But I will say this...you'd be surprised at how many successful athletes turn to people like me to discuss the mental challenges they face while trying to perform at a high level."

"So, talking to you helps them improve their jump shot?" Robert asked sarcastically.

"Noooo, I can't make a free throw myself." Dr. Miles smiled and gestured for Robert to sit. "I never discussed their technique. My job was to give them methods to block out the distractions that prevent *them* from improving their jump shot. Guys at that level face challenges that normal athletes don't. Outside pressures have ruined more careers than you'd think."

"I'll bet," Robert muttered and sat in the chair in front of the desk.

"Would you like something to drink? I have coffee, tea, and water."

A*N*IMUS

"No, thanks."

"Okay, well let's cut to the chase. I must admit, I was disappointed that you stopped coming to see me. Tell me why you stopped coming?"

"Truthfully?"

"Please."

"I stopped coming because I didn't see what good it was doing. I thought you were supposed to provide answers and all you did was ask questions. If I'm going to pay these rates, I need answers. Otherwise, I can deal with my problems on my own."

"Fair enough. I appreciate your honesty." Dr. Miles leaned back, placed his elbows on the arms of his leather chair, and steepled his hands at his chin. "So, tell me, have you been able to deal with the problem on your own?"

The loaded question made Robert defensive.

"Well, Doc, the fact that my wife called you should be an indication that nothing has changed."

"That's her opinion. I want to know your opinion."

"I'm in my forties and I'm still having dreams of killing my father. I'm no doctor, but I know that's not normal."

"Your concern with talking to me centered around me doing more listening than talking. It's a complaint I've heard a time or two during my career. I don't want my style to be the barrier between us, so I'm going to take a different approach today. Do you mind if I give *my* opinion?"

"If you think it'll help."

"I can't guarantee it will help, but I'll tell you what I think."

"Fire away."

"Okay, I will." Dr. Miles waited a beat before proceeding. "Have you ever heard of Post-Traumatic Stress Disorder (PTSD)?"

"Yes. A lot of my buddies were diagnosed with it after we returned from Afghanistan."

ANIMUS

"I see. Did you know the condition is not unique to soldiers? Anyone who has endured a frightening event or a stressful situation for an extended amount of time can develop it. As a child, you watched your father physically abuse your mother."

"And me."

"Right, and you. Now, more than thirty years later, you're having nightmares about it. Do you know what Sigmund Freud said about dreams?"

"No."

"Freud theorized that dreams are repressed desires. You were a child when the physical and emotional abuse happened. You were forced to stand by and watch it because you were too small to protect yourself or your mother. That had a deep psychological effect on you. Now that you are an adult and have your own family that you proudly protect, you think about the person who hurt you and seemingly got away with it."

"My dad."

"That's right...your dad." Dr. Miles snatched a tissue from the box on his desk, removed his glasses, and wiped the lenses with a slow, deliberate motion. "You've mentioned that he was physically abusive to you and your mother. Was there any other form of abuse?"

"What...like sexual abuse?"

"Yes."

"Nawh, he never did anything like that to me. It was just physical and verbal. He was very intimidating back then. He'd call me names and tell my mom I wasn't gon' be shit. Could you ever tell your own child that he wouldn't amount to shit?"

"No, I couldn't," Dr. Miles said calmly. "That's a very hurtful thing to say. I understand you own several businesses."

"Yeah."

"And you're a college graduate and a military veteran."

"Yes."

ANIMUS

"Do you see the correlation?"

"I never did before today. Are you saying that everything I've accomplished is because my dad said I wouldn't amount to shit?" Robert dismissed the thought. "Nawh, I ain't givin' his ass credit for nothing I've done. I can honestly say that I've never thought about him or wondered whether he'd be proud of me when I've accomplished anything in life."

Dr. Miles' smirk suggested he felt otherwise.

"You've given me examples of the physical and verbal abuse, but you didn't elaborate on how he was intimidating."

Robert had a far off look in his eyes. It was clear by the way he squinted and grimaced that he was traveling to a time and place that he would have preferred to forget.

"He looked like a giant to me back then."

"Is he as tall as you?"

"A little shorter—around six feet. Probably weighed about two hundred pounds when I was in elementary school. Now I see that's not a big man, but back then he appeared—"

"Huge."

"Yeah. Once I started to grow, I was still intimidated by him physically, but I was also afraid of his mind."

"How so?"

"He was…well, is…a smart man. A wizard at math. My mom once told me that he went to college to study accounting but dropped out. When I tell you, this man is smart at math…I'm talking mathematician level smarts. Accounting used to be his hustle. Our kitchen table used to be covered in tax paperwork at tax season. He used to do his friends' taxes—for a fee of course. When he wasn't doing his friends' taxes, he used to do the *books* for nightclubs owned by shady businessmen. I heard he once worked for the mob in New Orleans." Robert nibbled on his bottom lip. "The problem with having an abusive dad that is a genius at math—"

"He was hard on you when it came to math."

"Yep, hard as hell on me." Robert shook his head and gritted his teeth so hard that his jaw muscles flexed. "I used to

ANIMUS

fail math all through junior high school because I hated asking him to help me with my homework.

"I remember one time, I think I was in the seventh grade, I approached him and asked if he could help me with an algebra problem. It was around five in the evening when I approached...I can remember this shit like it was yesterday.

"He was a big gambler—lived at the racetrack betting on horse races—so when I approached, he was reading a racing form. He stopped to help me with my algebra problem. I made the mistake of not understanding his explanation right away and he looked at me like I was the gum on the bottom of his shoe. I immediately regretted asking him for help."

"What happened?"

"He rolled that racing form so tight that it was as stiff as a bat. He went over the problem again and asked me to take him through the steps I used to come up with that wrong answer I'd written down. Every time I messed up, he smacked me across my head with that racing form. Smack. Smack. Smack." Robert grimaced as if he could feel the blows. "The licks didn't necessarily hurt."

"It was the act that hurt," Dr. Miles said.

"Yeah. There was this look in his eyes. It's like he was swinging with all his might. Do you remember how the old folks used to hang a rug over a clothesline and beat it with a broom to get the dirt out?"

"Yes. My grandmother used to make me do it when I was a kid."

"That's how he beat me with that newspaper. Like he was trying to knock the dumbness out of me. The racing form would bend when it hit me. He would straighten it out and swing it again. He smacked me across my head with that racing form from five in the evening until ten thirty that night." Robert wasn't aware of it, but his eyes started to glisten. "He made my mama bring him his dinner and ate while watching me struggle with the algebra problems."

"Problems? I thought you said it was one problem?"

ANIMUS

"Oh, I forgot to mention, that one problem I asked him to help me with led him to creating five additional algebra problems for me to solve. I guess that was his way of making sure I understood how to do them."

Dr. Miles nodded and said, "Continue."

"He casually ate his food like he was at a restaurant. Then he'd stopped eating to check my answers. If I had one wrong, he'd grab that rolled up racing form and smack me across my head." Robert took a deep breath and exhaled. "I remember looking at my mom. I guess I hoped she'd tell him to stop, but she didn't. Truth be told, she couldn't. In hindsight, I'm glad she didn't come to my defense. There is no doubt in my mind that he would've used his paper bat to smack her upside the head too." Robert shrugged. "I didn't eat dinner that night; went to bed hungry."

"Did you answer the problems to his satisfaction?"

"Honestly, Doc, I don't even remember. All I know is, I was terrible at algebra throughout junior high and high school. Had to do a whole lot of cheating to make it through."

Dr. Miles nodded at the box of tissue. Robert grabbed a few pieces and dabbed his eyes and nose.

"Describe your relationship with your own kids."

"My little girls are the center of my world."

"Have you ever lost your temper with them and struck out?"

"I've never laid a finger on my daughters. I couldn't see myself hitting them." Robert reflexively glanced over his shoulder to make sure they were alone before he looked at the doctor and said, "Confession."

"Fire away."

"I'm ashamed to admit it, but I wasn't happy when Melody first told me she was pregnant. I never really wanted kids. Honestly, I was scared I might be the kind of father that he was. I had been in Afghanistan a few months. Our unit stayed in the middle of some type of conflict. Finally, I got a chance to call home after my second month over there. That's

ANIMUS

when she told me she was pregnant…with twins. The other soldiers standing around were happier than me." Robert looked ashamed. "Of course, I've never told Melody that."

"Your secret is safe with me."

"Good."

"The way you felt is not uncommon. It's rooted in the age-old nature vs. nurture debate."

"What do you mean?"

"It's a debate that's been around since the days of Plato. Do we act the way we do because we are genetically predisposed…meaning it's in our DNA? Or, do we act the way we do because of what we learn from our environment?"

"Like the whole gay topic. Are people born gay or do they act that way based on what they are exposed to?"

"Yes. Or, for example, does a child become a straight "A" student because of the DNA she inherits from her smart parents? That's nature. Or, does she become a straight "A" student because she's placed in an environment where education is a high priority and the tools for success are provided? That's nurture." Dr. Miles turned his chair sideways and draped one leg over the other. "It's not uncommon for people who grew up being abused to be concerned that they might have inherited that behavior. They are often the most hesitant to have kids of their own."

"What do you believe?"

"I believe the conversation is too deep to dive into during an hour-long session. However, I can tell you this—overcompensation is common with people who were abused. Do you tell your daughters you love them?"

"Several times a day."

"Are you real affectionate?"

Robert chuckled. "Yeah. I hug them every chance I get. They're both ten now, so they don't like it; always trying to pull away and wipe off my kisses."

"It's just a phase, don't take it personal. Kids start out seeking our affection when they are young. As they move into their teens, they detest our affection. And when they become adults, they become mature enough to appreciate our affection. Your girls will become clingy again. .trust me. The point I want to make is that you clearly give your girls the love and affection that you never received as a child."

"I get it."

"Now, the million-dollar question…have you and your father talked about what happened when you were a child?"

"No. When I left home at seventeen and went away to college, I never looked back. I was pretty good at basketball; good enough to earn a full scholarship to an HBCU."

"Where'd you go to school?"

"Southern University," Robert said proudly. "Honestly, I think I was more eager to get out of the house than play basketball. After I graduated college, I joined the military and stayed in for a little over six years."

"Thank you for your service."

"Thanks," Robert said, blowing through the compliment like it was a yellow light and he was late for work. "Once I got out of the military, I moved here to Dallas."

"Run much lately?" Dr. Miles asked sarcastically and smirked.

"You call it running, I call it starting over."

"Touché. However, I'd be remiss if I didn't point out that problems are like rashes…you can try to cover them up and put distance between yourself and them, but they'll continue to fester and itch until they are dealt with."

"So, you're saying I need to talk to my dad or else the dreams of killing him will continue?"

"I'm saying that your dreams of killing your father are a symptom; your ailment, is the physical and verbal abuse he inflicted on you when you were a child. No sickness has ever been cured by only addressing the symptom. If it were that simple, no one would have problems that linger." Dr. Miles adjusted his glasses, interlocked his fingers, and rocked back in

ANIMUS

his chair. "Your wife told me that your father is living with you because of Hurricane Katrina. Is that true?"

"Yes."

"As I've stated, he represents your ailment. Now that's he's under your roof do you plan on addressing your past with him?"

"You want me to make amends with the man I hate?"

"I didn't say make amends. That would suggest you did something wrong. I'm merely asking if you're going to use this time to talk to him about what happened. And as far as you *hating* him, that's an entirely different discussion."

"What do you mean?"

"Hate is an often-misused word."

"Well, Doc, you got a better word for what I feel?"

Dr. Miles strummed those tentacle-like fingers of his on the desk while he studied Robert. After a few seconds, the strumming stopped and he steepled his hands in front of his mouth. He peered over the wireframe glasses perched on the bridge of his nose and replied in a somewhat haunting tone.

"Robert, what you feel is best described as…animus."

"What?"

"Animus," Dr. Miles reiterated. "You see, hate is the byproduct of extreme dislike. But people don't always act on that feeling. Do you hate bigots?"

"Yes."

"Are you compelled to kill every bigot you encounter?"

"Of course not."

"That's good to know." Dr. Miles smiled. "Animus is also extreme dislike, but it looks a little different than hate. Animus deals with the impulses and actions produced by feelings of hate. When you have animus toward a person or thing, the desire to confront that person or thing is greater and more likely."

"Hence my dreams of killing my dad."

Dr. Miles nodded. "Which brings me back to my original question…are you going to sit down and talk to him?"

Animus

Robert rubbed the back of his neck, frowned, and crossed his arms while he stared out the window. Dr. Miles sized him up for a moment and then spoke directly.

"Robert, you stopped coming to see me after two visits because you didn't feel I was offering solutions. Well, I'm laying out a path for you and you don't want to give it a try."

"I didn't say I don't want to talk to him."

"You didn't have to say it, your body language is speaking loud and clear. The fidgeting in your seat. The frown. Crossing your arms—which is a reflexive action when we aren't ready to receive an idea or a person. It signals that you are closed to the idea of talking to him." Dr. Miles placed his elbows on his desk, intertwined his fingers, and leaned into his next remark. "Young man, the universe is talking to you. You went from New Orleans to Baton Rouge to Afghanistan and now you're here in Dallas. All of that moving around and the person you were trying to get away from has still shown up at your front door. Now, are you going to "man up" and talk to your father, or are you going to take the easy way out and throw him out of your house so that you don't have to address your ailment?"

"Since you put it like that, I guess I'll be talking to him."

"I'm simply *putting* it the way you *said* you wanted it…straight no chaser."

Robert thought for a moment. "I guess I'll talk to him, but I'm not ready to do it yet. I need some time to think about what I'm gonna say. Right now, all I wanna do is choke him every time I see him. Any advice on what I should say?"

"First, you're going to have to control your temper when you talk to him. Choking the man is not an option. As far as *what* you should say—that'll come to you. I do think it would be wise to start the conversation by asking him why he did the things he did. Give him a chance to explain without interruption. And finish the conversation with letting him know how his actions affected you."

ANIMUS

"I hear you." Robert inhaled and exhaled with a hiss. "Well, this wasn't what I expected."

"Are you glad you came?"

"Honestly, I am," Robert smiled.

"Good." Dr. Miles stood up and extended his hand. "Can I expect to see you next month?"

Robert shook Dr. Miles' hand and said, "Don't push it, Doc."

15

Gloria continued to stew after her run-in with Enis. Like an angry drill sergeant, she barged into the bedroom where the boys slept and started raising hell. The only thing she didn't have was a metal garbage can and lid to clang like cymbals to get their attention.

"Time to get up, get dressed, and clean this smelly room!"

The young lads raised their heads like meerkats sensing danger. They yawned, grumbled, and stretched while rising. Once their vision cleared and they were aware of their surroundings, they stumbled over each other while gathering their clothes. They were very respectful, so they didn't offer any overt protest to the fiery Latina's order, but they mumbled their displeasure.

ANIMUS

"I don't know what you do at your house, but here, we clean." Gloria grabbed a pair of tennis shoes. "This room smells. You...what's your name?"

"Jalen."

"Are you the oldest?"

"Yes, ma'am."

"These your brothers?"

"Yes, ma'am."

"Okay, you're in charge. I want you to get them cleaned up and then you all come to the kitchen. I'll fix breakfast." Gloria kicked a pair of shorts. "And then after you eat, you come and clean up this room. From top to bottom, I want it cleaned."

"Yes, ma'am."

Gloria walked out of the room and bumped into EJ.

"Ms. Gloria are you okay?"

"No! That room stinks." And then, as if she remembered what set her off to begin with, she pointed at EJ. "And your papa should not be in Mr. Rob's office!"

"Yes, ma'am. I told him it was wrong to do that. It won't happen again."

"Better not. Or I tell Mr. Rob." She headed down the stairs and toward the kitchen. EJ had to shuffle to keep up. "Mr. Rob told me no one go in his office," Gloria's English worsened as her anger grew. "Only me and Mrs. Mel. That's it."

"Yes, ma'am."

"You wanna eat?" She tossed the question over her shoulder at Rob. "I fix a lot to feed everyone."

"No, ma'am."

"What about your papa?"

"No, ma'am. We're about to leave."

"I gotta cook breakfast for those boys and clean up. It's dirty, dirty, dirty."

EJ looked around. Compared to his house, Robert's house was spotless. Nevertheless, he continued to let her rant without challenge. Ultimately, he needed to make sure she didn't mention anything to his brother. If he challenged her in any way, she might tell Robert what she noticed. Hell, hath no fury, like Ms. Gloria scorned.

Enis entered the living room, but Ms. Gloria was looking in the refrigerator and didn't notice him. EJ placed a finger over his lips and pointed at the front door.

"Okay, Ms. Gloria, me and my dad are going to go and see about getting him some assistance."

Gloria threw up her hand to acknowledge she'd heard him but continued to examine the contents of the refrigerator and talk to herself.

"I've got to clean refrigerator too. Everything is dirty, dirty, dirty."

"Is she always like that?" Enis asked as they got into the car.

"Shhiii," EJ rammed the key into the ignition, "today is one of her good days."

The line outside of the McKinney branch of the Red Cross was wrapped around the block. People of all races waited patiently for their turns to enter the tiny building to receive the assistance that would kickstart their road to recovery. Some wore tattered clothes. Some wore shirts that still had the "fresh off the shelf" creases down the middle. What they all had in common was a shared look of anxiousness.

"Damn, that line is long," EJ said. "Are all these people from Louisiana?"

"Son, over five hundred thousand people had to evacuate the state. Half of that number came from the New Orleans area. I'm surprised the line isn't longer."

EJ sighed. "I guess I'd better find somewhere to park so you can hurry up and get in line."

"No, you don't. Pull up in front of the building and keep the car running. I'll be right back."

EJ let Enis out on the sidewalk near the front entrance and watched him hobble across the grass and straight through

ANIMUS

the front door. Moments later, Enis hobbled back out with a handful of literature.

"C'mon, let's go."

"Go where?"

"To get something to eat. I'm hungry."

"Un-uh. Rob told me to get you here so you can take care of your business. I told you he wants proof that you are doing what you need to do to get back on your feet. I'm gon' say it again...he wants you out of his house."

"Here's the damn proof that I was here," Enis barked and held up the Red Cross brochures. "Now, take me to that IHOP we passed on the way here."

"And then we're coming back?"

"Nope. After we eat, we're gonna drive up to that casino that's an hour away. The one that's right past the Oklahoma border."

"WinStar?"

"Yep."

"No. Rob's already pissed at me. I'm bringing you—"

"To the damn casino," Enis said. "Don't you like money?"

"Of course."

"Didn't you say Darlene has been stressing you out about getting some down payment money for a house?"

"Yeah."

"Didn't I tell you I had a plan to get paid, and when I do, I was gon' break bread with you?"

"Yeah."

"Then shut the hell up and drive this piece of shit to IHOP like I told you to, boy!"

EJ rolled his eyes, took his foot off the brake, toggled between the gas pedal and the clutch, and put the car in gear. The Mitsubishi Eclipse jerked and then they sped away like they'd robbed a bank.

Unbeknownst to EJ and Enis, Melody and Kim were standing in the long winding line. Melody didn't know it was

ANIMUS

Enis, and she didn't heckle the limping man like many of the other angst-filled people who wondered aloud if he'd lost his damn mind, but she did mumble their sentiments. It wasn't until he returned to the car and she noticed the pronounced limp that she realized the man was her father-in-law.

Kim was too busy babbling about the items she needed to purchase later at Target to pay attention to Enis, but she noticed Melody wasn't paying attention to her. She followed Melody's gaze but was still unsure of what had snatched her sister's attention.

"Mel, what are you lookin' at?".

Melody squinted. "That looks like EJ and Enis."

"Where?"

"Driving away in that burgundy car."

It was close to three o'clock when EJ and Enis returned from their day of screwing off. As they drove along I-35 to Hwy 380 they rehearsed what they'd say to Robert once he started peppering them with questions about their whereabouts. They bickered and debated about what to say and how to say it, but by the time they pulled into Robert's driveway, they were on the same page.

"Is that one of y'all company trucks?"

"Nawh. Rob must be having some work done at his house today." EJ pulled into Robert's driveway. He put the car in neutral and returned to the primary topic of discussion. "Are we straight? Because Rob don't miss much. He's gon' peep game if our stories don't add up."

"Boy, pull down your skirt. I got this."

Enis and EJ exchanged fist bumps. Enis gathered his paraphernalia and exited the car. EJ backed up and sped away.

A man exited the truck parked at the edge of the driveway. He wore a t-shirt that looked like he had to squeeze

ANIMUS

into it, jeans, and a baseball cap that was pulled down to his eyebrows.

"Is this the Sumina residence?"

"Yeah, who's asking?"

The man adjusted his hat and flashed a gold-toothed smile. "Remember me?"

How could Enis forget? It was the man who caused the wound in his leg; a wound that smarted with every step he took. Enis looked over the man's shoulder and saw another man walking toward him.

"Booker! What you doin' here?"

"Enis, you don't look happy to see me."

"Nawh, that's not it. I'm…I'm just surprised to see you. It's not the ninth."

"I don't know why you're surprised to see me. You think you're the only person who can evacuate to Texas? I told you I had people here." Booker removed his shades. "As far as it not being the ninth of the month…I know it's not. Technically, you still have four days to get my money. But I haven't heard from you in a minute and thought I'd pay you a visit since I was in the area." Booker surveyed Robert's house and the immaculate landscaping. "Damn E, you weren't lying about your son. He must be paid. This is a fire ass crib."

Enis could feel more than Booker's goon's eyes zeroed in on him. He looked back at the house, and just as he expected, Gloria was posted in the window looking at them.

"Look man," Enis said in a low voice, "I said I'd have your money and I meant it. Don't come…"

Booker's sly grin turned into a scowl. Letting Enis know he needed to choose his words carefully.

"…I mean, please don't come here again."

Booker waved at Gloria.

"Alright, I'll leave. I know when I'm not welcomed." He wagged his finger at Enis. "Four days, E. The clock is ticking. Have my money in four days or," he pointed at Mr. Thick Arms, "my man here is gon' have to pay you a visit."

ANIMUS

The goon lifted the front of his shirt to show the butt of a pistol.

"C'mon, let's bounce," Booker said.

Booker and his companion went back to the truck and drove away. Enis stood at the end of the driveway and watched them until they turned the corner. When he turned to go inside, he noticed Gloria was no longer in the window.

Enis entered the house hoping to avoid Gloria and make it to his bedroom, but that wasn't the case.

"You in trouble. And you bring trouble to Mr. Rob's home." She shook her head in disgust. "You're a bad man." She patted her chest. "I feel it."

Enis watched the woman as she ascended the stairs. His instincts told him that Gloria could be more of a problem than he anticipated.

16

Melody and Kim walked out of Target with wide smiles. They both pushed red shopping carts that struggled to hold white shopping bags. Melody dropped the third-row seat of the SUV and they tossed the bags inside.

Melody glanced at her wristwatch. "We finished with just enough time to make it to the girl's school before they let out."

The line of cars outside the school was almost as long as the line outside the Red Cross building. Faith and Hope stood with their hands on their bony hips and their backs to the curb. Their long plaits swayed rhythmically as they rolled their necks and pointed their fingers in a boy's face.

"Is that Faith and Hope?"

"Yeah, that's them."

"Why does it look like they're yelling at that boy?"

ANIMUS

"Because they are. That's the same little boy Rob and I had to meet with the principal about." Melody pulled alongside the curb, honked, and lowered the window. "Faith! Hope! Y'all come on!"

The girls spun on their heels and climbed in the SUV.

"What were y'all tellin' that child?" asked Kim. "He looks like he's about to cry?"

"He was tellin' people I cheated on my test because I got a better grade than him," Faith said.

"I heard him tellin' that to Ginny and Freddie," Hope said. "So, I told him my sister don't have to cheat to get a better grade than his stupid self."

"I told you," Melody said, "she can mess with her sister, but nobody else can."

"I see," Kim replied, and contorted her body so that she could see the girls better. "What were y'all saying to him when we pulled up?"

"I told him that if he talked about my sister again, I was going to tell my daddy that he hit me and then my daddy would beat up his daddy."

"He shut up then," Faith said and laughed.

Kim turned around and looked out the front window. A smile emerged on her face.

"I don't want y'all to act like bullies," Melody said.

"But mama, he started!" Hope said.

"I know that, but y'all need to learn to ignore him. And stop threatening that child by telling him you're going to have your dad beat up his dad."

"Well, he did have it coming," Kim mumbled.

"You're so messy," Melody said.

Kim smiled and shrugged.

Melody stopped at Chick-Fil-A and bought enough food to feed a football team. By the time they made it to the house, Gloria was gone for the day but there was no denying she'd been there. The scent of bleach floated from the kitchen to the front door.

ANIMUS

"Did someone spill bleach?" Kim asked as they entered the house.

"That's Gloria's calling card, girl. She is old school. She doesn't even bother with all the cleaning supplies I have in the laundry room. All she uses is bleach and hot water. She wipes every inch of the kitchen with it."

"At least you know everything is sterilized," Kim said. "Jalen, Johnny, and Josh! Y'all come and get these bags out of the car!"

"They're outside, Tee-Kim," Faith said, pointing at the patio.

Kim walked out on to the back patio. Two mountain bikes were turned upside down. The wheels were off, and the chains were sprawled on the patio.

"What y'all doing out here?"

"Mr. Enis found these bikes in the back of Uncle Rob's shed," Josh said. "The only thing wrong with them is that they have flat tires."

"Mr. Enis is showing us how to patch a tire and fix the chains," Johnny added.

Enis and Jalen were on their knees examining an inner tube. Johnny and Josh stood over their shoulders listening intently to the old man's every instruction.

"Yeah, apply it just like that," Enis said, watching Jalen apply glue to the square patch and then monitoring the way he placed it on the deflated inner tube. "You've gotta let it dry for a few minutes to make sure it gets a good seal before you put air in it."

"Y'all need to come and get these bags out of the truck, and then y'all can eat. We got some Chick-Fil-A in here. You hungry Mr. Enis?"

"Nawh, I'm good for now, baaaby. Thanks."

Kim returned to the kitchen.

"What are they doing out there?"

"They found some old bikes in your shed. Mr. Enis is showing them how to patch a flat or something."

ANIMUS

"Girl, Rob bought those bikes for us two years ago. We were supposed to go riding together once a week to get in better shape. That lasted one month. We both got flat tires on the same day. We ain't touched those bikes since."

"Well, they're getting *touched* now." Kim looked at the boys through the window. "I can't lie, when I see them like that, it makes me sad. I know they miss having a man around. That's the kind of stuff their dad should be teaching them how to do."

"It's alright, Sis," Melody said and draped her arm around Kim. "You've done a hell of a job raising them on your own."

"Yeah, but I can only teach them so much. It takes a man to teach boys how to be men. I miss Jalen so much."

"I know you do. He's watching down on you and the boys."

Kim nodded in agreement. She sighed and dabbed her eyes. "I've gotta be honest, Sis. I know Rob has a problem with his dad, but he doesn't seem that bad. I'm not saying he didn't do hurtful things in the past, but since he's been here, all I've seen him doing is trying to help y'all."

"You can't tell Rob that. All he sees is a man that caused him pain."

"Maybe that's why Enis is being so helpful," Kim said. She removed the food from the bags and shoved one of the waffle fries into her mouth. "Girl, when you think you're about to die, your whole perspective on life changes. When that flood water was rising, all I could do was pray and ask God to get us out of there. You start thinking about all the shit you've done wrong and how you'd do things differently if you get a second chance. Maybe Enis views this as his second chance."

Melody watched her father-in-law through the window and said, "Yeah, maybe you're right. People make mistakes and they can change. The problem is, convincing the people they've already hurt that they've really changed." Melody shook off the trance and looked at Kim. "You know what, this

128

ANIMUS

conversation is depressing. We're going to feed these kids and then go have a little retail therapy to get our minds right."

"But we just finished shopping."

"That was for stuff to put in your house. I'm taking you to the mall to do some real shopping."

EJ walked into his house feeling more exhausted than he would've been had he gone to work. All he wanted was an ice-cold beer and a hot meal. He'd gone to the grocery store the night before, so he was confident that a cold beer awaited. But the only scent that lurked in his house was weed.

"What are you doing?"

"What does it look like I'm doing?"

"It looks like you're sitting there smoking a blunt. Didn't you just tell me you are pregnant?"

"Yes, I did. This baby is barely the size of a pea. A little weed ain't gon' hurt."

"Dee, put the damn weed out!"

Darlene rolled her eyes and smashed the blunt in the ashtray. EJ was tempted to call her stupid but decided he didn't have the energy to put up with the fight that would ensue. Instead, he grabbed a beer from the refrigerator.

"Did you cook?"

"Do you see anything on the stove?"

"I made groceries last night. We got shoulder blade steaks, pork chops, ground meat...all kinds of stuff in here to cook. What you been doin' all day?"

"Dealing with a stove that won't work. The circuit keeps tripping." Darlene shrugged. "Can't cook on an electric stove if it won't stay on. We wouldn't have to deal with this if you," Darlene looked at EJ and raised her voice up two octaves, "did what you said you was gon' do and bought me a goddamn new house!"

"Stupid ass," EJ hissed and ripped the cap off the beer.

ANIMUS

"Where you been all day? When the circuit breaker kept trippin' I called your cellphone but you didn't answer. I called your office and they said you went home." Darlene walked over to EJ and stood close enough to smell his breath. "You ain't been here, so where you been?"

"Girl, get outta my face."

Darlene grabbed his belt buckle and unbuckled his pants. When his pants loosened, she rammed her hand inside of his drawers and gripped his penis and balls.

"Aww, shit!" EJ yelled. Beer spilled from his mouth. "What the fuck are you doin'?"

"Nigga if you move, I'm gon' squeeze these ma'fucka's 'til they pop." Darlene said through pressed lips. "When I'm finished inspecting you, you can move."

"Alright, alright, I ain't movin'."

Darlene fondled his balls and squeezed his penis for nearly ten seconds. She pulled her hand out of his pants and smelled the palm.

"Yo' ass is crazy!" EJ said. He leaned over the chair and groaned. "Ghetto ass."

"Aww quit actin' like a lil bitch. I didn't even squeeze that hard."

"You don't have to squeeze a man's balls to hurt 'em. All you gotta do is graze balls."

"Did you buy peas last night?"

"What?"

"Did you buy peas, nigga!"

"Yeah!"

"Then press a bag of cold peas against your balls. You're lucky your dick and balls don't smell like pussy." Darlene walked back over to the sofa and grabbed the television remote. "Now answer my question...where you been all day?"

"With my daddy."

"Doin' what?"

ANIMUS

"Rob made me take him over to the Red Cross to get assistance."

"Did he get everything he needs?"

"No."

"Why?"

"Because he don't plan on needin' it."

Darlene put the remote down and looked at EJ. She cocked her head slightly and gave him the side-eye.

"Let me get this straight…your daddy loses everything in the storm. He comes to Dallas and moves in with the son who hates his guts. The son also happens to be rich. Rich son wants dad out of his house. Rich son tells you—the brother he blames for bringing the dad around—to go help the dad get Red Cross assistance. Stupid son—you—says dad refused assistance because he ain't gon' need it. But we all know it's gon' be months before New Orleans opens back up. So, why wouldn't dad want Red Cross assistance?" Darlene stared at the floor. Her facial expressions changed repeatedly as she tried to do the math in her head. Once she'd solved the problem, she looked at EJ and stood up. "Oooh, you sneaky ma'fucka." She pointed at EJ. "Rob gon' beat both y'all ass."

"Shut up. You don't know what you talkin' 'bout."

"I know when a nigga gon' lose some teeth. You must've forgot, I ain't no bougie bitch like ya sista-in-law. I'm from the 'hood. I can spot a hustle from a mile away." She clapped her hands as she walked toward the bedroom. "Yeesss, indeed. I don't even wanna know the details. Either way, a bitch gon' get paid. If y'all pull it off, we gon' come up. If y'all don't pull it off and Rob kills yo' ass, that insurance policy I have on you gon' pay off. Shiii…this is a win-win for me."

17

September 5, 2005/McKinney, TX.
6:55 p.m.

Melody and Kim left out of the Stonebriar Mall grinning like two Cheshire Cats. They'd put the "retail" in retail therapy, and if the looks on their faces were any indication—it felt damn good.

"Girl, I don't know how I'm going to pay you back for all of this," Kim said as she climbed in the car.

"Give me some time to think about it, I'll come up with something."

"I bet you will," Kim replied.

They stopped at Starbucks on the way home and grabbed two overpriced coffees. Melody then took the scenic route through a few ritzy neighborhoods, making it a point to pass in front of the high school.

"Damn. The campus is huge."

Melody couldn't show her delight, but she wasn't about to let the moment pass without pitching her little sister again. "I told you they do it big out here. The cheapest house in this neighborhood is probably four hundred thousand. The most expensive is probably around six hundred thousand. Schools are primarily funded by property taxes. Trust me, when you consider how much property taxes we pay around here, these white folks would lose their mind if these high school campuses weren't the size of your average HBCU."

"I know that's right," Kim mumbled.

"Are the boys still into baseball?"

"Girl, they eat, sleep, and breathe baseball."

Melody pointed at the baseball field located in the far corner of the campus. "That's the baseball field. And see that football field next to it?"

"Yeah."

"That's the outdoor field that the football team practices on."

"That looks like Pan Am stadium. You remember Pan Am stadium next to Bayou St. John?"

Melody smiled. "Girl, how could I forget? Remember how them fools used to fight in the parking lot after games?"

"Every damn game," Kim said. "Everybody used to climb to the top bleachers and look down into the parking lot and laugh while those fools went at it. Twenty on twenty…all that white dust in the air from the gravel in the parking lot."

"Yeah, it was funny until the gun shots started ringing out," Melody said.

"I know that's right. Everybody that was watching from the top bleachers started scurrying like roaches. A bullet ain't got no name."

"We've been out here for over a decade, and I have never heard a gunshot."

ANIMUS

Kim sipped her coffee and nodded. As much as she hated to admit it, her boys would have a much better quality of life in the suburbs of Dallas than in the hard streets of New Orleans. Every time they left the house in the Big Easy, she worried that they wouldn't return. She cringed whenever they asked for expensive shoes or clothing, knowing that they'd become a target for thugs. The fact that the Orleans Parish School District had to mandate uniforms because kids were being robbed for their clothing was enough for any parent to want to find a safer environment. So, why was she so eager to get back to New Orleans? Was it just because she was homesick? Isn't the well-being of your kids supposed to trump an adult's desires? Why was her every waking thought centered around going back to the Crescent City as soon as she could, rather than embracing all that the suburbs had to offer?

"I hear you, Sis," Kim muttered. "I hear you."

Feeling like she'd won that round, Melody headed home. She'd promised the kids that she'd fry shrimp and catfish and make po'boys and knew that if she didn't get started on their meal, they'd raid her refrigerator in search of anything they could find.

"How is Rob doing? Every time his dad comes around, he looks like he wants to beat the hell out of the man."

"Girl, you hit the nail on the head." Melody increased her speed on Lake Forest Drive. "I'm trying to get home now because I hate leaving those two alone. Robert has so much anger in his heart toward that man. Don't get me wrong, Enis has done some foul shit, but I'm just saying…we've been preaching to our kids the importance of forgiveness. How does it look if their dad can't even forgive his own father?"

Melody arrived home in record time. They walked in the house carrying bags like it was Black Friday. None of the kids acknowledged their presence because they were all on their hands and knees peering under the sofa, behind the sofa, and searching between sofa cushions.

"What are y'all doing?" Kim asked.

ANIMUS

"Lookin' for Mr. Enis' watch," Josh said.

Enis entered the kitchen. "Yeah, the kids were helping me look for my watch. I seemed to have misplaced it. I've had it for years. It's one of the few mementos my dad left me."

"Where did you last see it?"

"I looked at it after I got back from the Red Cross today."

"I thought that was you and EJ I saw today."

"Yeah, I was out there." Enis looked down at the kitchen floor and between the bar stools. "I must've misplaced it somewhere between the kitchen, living room, and my bedroom. I don't go upstairs, so I know it's not up there." He rubbed the back of his neck and frowned as if he needed a massage. "It ain't much, but it was important to me. I ain't like you, daughter-in-law…I don't have Rolex watches that I can just let people wear. I need my little raggedy watch."

"What are you talkin' 'bout? I don't let people wear my Rolex."

Enis stood still like a child who'd revealed a secret.

"Enis, what are you talking about?"

Enis made sure the kids weren't listening and then he moved over to the kitchen counter, beckoning Melody to follow him.

"Umm, I don't know how to say this."

"Say what?"

"That housekeeper…"

"Yeah, Gloria. What about her?"

"I saw her coming out of your bedroom today."

"She's allowed to go in there and clean up."

"I figured that, but is she allowed to try on your jewelry? Because I saw her wearing an expensive watch when she came out of your bedroom today. I ain't no watch connoisseur, but I know a Rolex when I see one."

Melody looked at Kim and then walked swiftly to her bedroom. Moments later, she returned to the kitchen.

"What's wrong?" Kim asked.

135

ANIMUS

"My Rolex is missing."

"Are you serious?"

"Dead serious."

"Has she ever stolen something before?"

"No, we've never had that kind of problem with her. She's always been trustworthy—if she weren't, I wouldn't have given her a key to my house."

"Are you going to tell Rob?"

"I don't know. Where is he?"

"He's in his office," Enis said.

Melody thought for a moment and then said, "I'll tell him, but not just yet."

"You're going to see her again," Kim said. "You can just ask her when she comes back to work, right?"

"She works Mondays and Thursdays."

"That's too long to wait," Kim said.

"I agree." Melody looked at Kim. "You wanna take a ride?"

"Bitch, you know I'm always down to take a ride."

"Let's get these kids situated first. Enis, thanks for telling me about this. And I'm sorry about your watch. I hope you find it."

While Melody and Kim were busy getting the kids situated, Enis stuck his head inside Robert's home office. "You got a second?"

"Yeah," Robert replied unenthusiastically without bothering to look at him.

Enis entered. His admired the huge built-in bookcase that took up one of the four walls and then looked at the adjacent wall which was covered in framed diplomas, certificates, and military memorabilia.

"Wow, this is impressive. Hell, if I had an office like this, I wouldn't come out either." Enis walked over to the

ANIMUS

bookshelf. "What Makes the Great, Great, by Dennis Kimbro. The Seven Habits of Highly Effective People, by Stephen Covey. Good to Great by Jim Collins. I see why you've accomplished all that you have, son." He surveyed the other books on the shelves. "I don't believe I've ever read anything thicker than a racing form. You really read all these books?"

Robert could hear Dr. Miles' voice in his ear: *Don't lose your temper.* But when Enis mentioned a racing form, it triggered all the pain Robert felt that night when he asked for help with his algebra homework.

"You actually read those racing forms? I thought you only used them as paper bats."

Enis pretended to not hear Robert's snide remark. He moseyed over to the wall with the diplomas and memorabilia. He studied Robert's diplomas and plaques, but his head stiffened when he spotted the most impressive, framed item.

"Damn, son, I never knew you won a Silver Star." Enis sounded genuinely impressed. "This is to certify that the President of the United States of America by Act of Congress has awarded the Silver Star medal to Lieutenant Robert L. Sumina for gallantry in action." Enis stared at Robert, who was still looking down at the paperwork on his desk. "Son, this is impressive. I mean yeah, I served during Vietnam, but I never did anything worth writing home about. You won a Silver Star. I've got goosebumps right now." Enis looked at his forearm as if trying to spot proof of his hyperbole. "I'm really impressed."

"What do you want?"

"Umm, I just came in to apologize."

"For coming to my house and disturbing my peace?"

"I didn't mean to disturb your peace. And I'm going to be getting out of your house soon. I'm working with the Red Cross and VA to get some accommodations. EJ brought me over there today."

"Good."

"Right now, I just wanna apologize to you for the pain I caused. I know that back in the day, I did your mama, and

ANIMUS

you, wrong. I was a different man back then. For starters, I wanna apologize for your name."

"What?"

"Your name. Haven't you ever wondered why your name is Robert and not Enis? After all, it's an unwritten rule that men name their first-born son after them."

The thought had crossed Robert's mind often when he was a younger man. Melody even asked him once, but since he didn't have an answer, he changed the topic. Since Enis decided to bring it up, now seemed like as good of a time as any to get an answer.

"Not that I care, but why didn't you name me after you?"

"Truthfully, I didn't name you after me because when your mama told me she was pregnant with you, I questioned whether you were mine."

"What!"

"It's the truth. She and I had separated for a few months and shortly after we got back together, she told me she was pregnant. I'd been hearing a few things around town, nothing I could confirm, so I went with it. But I always wondered if you were mine."

Robert stood up. "What are you tryin' to say about my mother?"

Enis started to answer but paused when he heard Melody in the hallway barking orders at the girls. Right as he was about to answer there was a knock at the door.

"Baby, me and Kim are about to take a quick ride. I'm leaving the girls here. The boys are down at the park playing basketball. Do you want something?"

"No, thanks. I'm good!" Robert shouted.

"Okay. My phone is about to die, so you may not be able to reach me until it recharges. We shouldn't be gone too long."

ANIMUS

Enis' body stiffened like a burglar fearful of being spotted in the shadows. He waited until it sounded like Melody had moved away from the door and then he continued.

"Back then son, I was an insecure man. I had just gotten out of the army. My money wasn't right. I couldn't find a decent job. I was always stressed out. On top of all of that, I was insecure. Your mama was so beautiful. Men used to flirt with her all the time. She never flirted back," Enis added, "but that didn't stop them from flirting with her.

"It was my insecurity that made me think you weren't mine. That insecurity also made me do a lot of the terrible things that I did to her. It was about control for me back then. I just wanted to control her. The only tool I had to control her was fear," Enis smirked, "and it worked. When I said jump, she asked how high. She did whatever I wanted her to do. Especially, in the bedroom."

That rage that swirled within Robert erupted like Mount Vesuvius. He lunged and used his left hand to clamp on to Enis' neck. Robert drove his father back to the wall so hard that many of the framed pictures fell. Robert used his leverage to keep Enis pressed against the wall.

"You lowdown bastard! I knew you hadn't changed!"

Robert swung his right fist the way a blacksmith wields a sledgehammer. Three decades of suppressed rage fueled the blow that struck Enis square in the jaw. Enis' face seemed to crumple from the impact and his body folded like an inflatable bouncer after the air has been let out. When his head smacked the floor, blood shot from his mouth. A second later, more blood spilled, but this time it came from his nose after Robert straddled him, gripped his throat with his left hand, and landed a second blow.

"This is for the day you beat my mother in front of my school and all of my friends watched." Robert gritted his teeth and raised his fist again. "This is for the time you beat me so bad that you sprain my arm and thumb." Robert struck him again. Each blow he landed felt better than the last.

ANIMUS

"I'm sorry!" Enis cried out. "I'm sorry, son!"

"Daddy!" Hope shouted from the doorway. Tears streaked down the child's face. "Stop hitting Granddaddy!" Faith stood behind her sister, gnawing at her fingernails while her body trembled like a leaf on a tree. She held the phone pressed to her ear.

"Daddy, please stop!" Hope shouted again.

Robert noticed the terror in his daughters' eyes, so he released Enis' throat and left the seemingly lifeless man on the floor in a puddle of his own blood. By this time, Robert was panting. His heart felt like it was about to burst through his chest. He stared down at the man whose abusive behavior caused him to urinate on himself many nights as a child. The man whom he often thought about poisoning with the rat poison that was kept under their kitchen sink.

"Look at'cha, crying like a little bitch." Robert kicked Enis in the ribs. "Nigga, you're only sorry that I remember all of the foul shit you did."

18

The east side of McKinney was home to a large Hispanic population. Laborers, most of whom could be credited with building the numerous subdivisions that now dotted the city's landscape, lived in houses that rivaled the wood framed houses that perished in the flood waters produced by Hurricane Katrina.

Gloria Valdez lived in a well-kept two-bedroom box home located on the edge of town. The front yard looked like a golf course. The shrubs were trimmed and the flowerbed outside the entrance was adorned with begonias. Inside the tiny abode, the scent of tortillas mingled with the breeze coming through a side window.

Gloria monitored the skillet with one eye to make sure the tortillas didn't get too dark; while the other eye remained glued to the soap opera she watched on Telemundo.

ANIMUS

"Don't believe him, Maria! Canelo don't love you. He's in love with your sister!"

Gloria's face crinkled as the character named Maria ignored her warning and dove into the arms of the man named Canelo.

"Stupid! She never listens!"

Before Gloria could continue to chastise the woman on the television screen, she thought she heard a knock at her front door. She flinched when the second knock happened. She turned down the television and turned off the burner on the stove and walked over to the front window next to the door. Visitors, especially that time of day, were seldom. The look of concern on her face vanished when she peeked out the curtain and saw Melody.

"Mrs. Mel!" Gloria said as she opened the front door.

"Hi, Ms. Gloria." Melody gestured at Kim. "This is my sister, Kim."

Gloria and Kim exchanged head nods.

"Is something wrong?"

"No," Melody said.

"Yes," Kim said.

Gloria appeared perplexed.

"Well, I'm not sure if something is wrong," Melody said. "I came over to talk to you. Can we come in for a moment?"

"Sure, sure," Gloria waved them in. "Please, sit down."

"It smells good in here," Melody said.

"I'm cooking huevos rancheros. Do you want some?"

"No, thank you. We won't stay long."

"Give me a second," Gloria said and scurried into the kitchen.

Melody and Kim examined their surroundings.

"This is a nice little place. Y'all pay her enough to afford this?"

"This is our house."

"What?"

ANIMUS

"You heard me...we own this house."

"Y'all gave it to her?"

"Not exactly. Initially, Robert bought it as a fixer-upper that we could flip. During that time, Gloria lived with another Mexican family in South Dallas. But that wasn't working out. On top of that, South Dallas is 30 to 40 minutes from us—it was too hard to check on her. The only other option she had was to go back to Mexico because she's an illegal alien and none of us wanted that. So, after Rob fixed up this place, we decided it would be a good little spot for Gloria. She could have her own space and not have to worry about rent. And she is close enough to us that she can make it back and forth to our house in her little car with no problem."

"Let me guess, y'all bought that little red car out there for her too."

"Yeah. We only paid a thousand dollars for it. Rob and EJ fixed whatever was wrong with it and we gave it to her so she can have transportation since there is no public transportation out here."

"That's another thing New Orleans has over McKinney. You can get around the whole city of New Orleans on a bus or the street cars. You need a car to go anywhere out here."

"I can't argue with that."

"Y'all sure have done a lot for this old lady. Rob must really feel indebted to her son."

"He is...and so am I. Their unit was somewhere in the desert chasing Saddam Hussein. It was late night and most of the soldiers were sleeping, but Robert and Sergeant Valdez— that was Gloria's son—were up playing cards. A grenade or something explosive was tossed into their tent. Sergeant Valdez saw it before Robert did. He saved Robert by pushing him out of the way, but he wasn't so lucky. The explosion took off Valdez's left leg. He bled to death. Right before he died, he asked Robert to take care of his mother and make sure she doesn't get deported." Melody looked around at the cottage. "I guess you can say this is what "taking care of his mother" looks like."

"Okay, now I understand. But what I don't understand is how she could steal from you after all that you've done for her."

"I don't get it either. Like I said, we've never had a problem with her roaming around in our house. She knows that if she needs anything, all she has to do is ask me or Rob and we'd give it to her. Honestly, she doesn't ask us for hardly anything. I just find it hard to believe that she would steal from me."

"Well, there's only one way to find out. We gon' look in her purse."

"What if it's not in the purse?"

"Then we gon' search the house."

"We can't just search her house."

"Umm, this is your house. You can search whatever the hell you want."

"No, I can't Kim. What if she says *no*?"

"Then you're going to threaten to call the Immigration Office and have her ass shipped back to the land of the big tacos."

"Land of the big tacos…really Kim."

"Tacos. Doritos. Whatever they eat in Mexico."

"I brought you some tea," Gloria said, emerging from the kitchen holding a tray. "I made it with the lemons I grow out back."

"Thank you," Melody said.

Melody and Kim sat on the sofa. Gloria placed the tray on the coffee table and sat in a claw foot chair across from the sofa.

"Tell me Mrs. Mel, what brings you here today?"

Melody looked at Kim. Kim's eyebrows arched as if to say: *Don't look at me. Tell her.*

ANIMUS

"Ms. Gloria, I'm not going to waste your time. I came here today to ask you about something that is missing from my house."

"Her four-thousand-dollar Rolex watch," Kim blurted out. "Have you seen it?"

"You mean the fancy gold and silver watch?"

"Yes," Melody said. "I keep it in my jewelry box on top of my dresser."

"I know. I've seen it when I clean up. Is it missing?"

"Yes. It's not where I put it. When did you last see it?"

Gloria thought for a moment and then shrugged. "I don't know. I didn't see it today when I was cleaning your bedroom."

"Are you sure?" Kim asked.

The question earned Kim a side-eye glare from Gloria. Kim rolled her neck and glared back.

"Umm, Ms. Gloria. I was wondering if—"

"You think I took it?" Gloria grabbed her imaginary pearls. "I don't steal!"

"Ms. Gloria, I'm not accusing you of stealing. I just want to—"

"Here, I show you my purse." Gloria walked over to a table next to her front door and grabbed her purse. "I keep everything in this purse. You can search it."

The purse landed on the coffee table with a thud. Its mouth yawned wide enough that the contents could be seen from where Melody and Kim sat.

"Mel, do you see what I see?" Kim mumbled.

"Yes, I do." Melody reached inside the purse cautiously, as if she expected the mouth to slam and trap her hand inside. She pulled out the stainless-steel watch with the 18-karat yellow gold fluted bezel and held it up like it was a worm. "How do you explain this?"

"Yeah, how do you explain that?"

Gloria's jaw hit the floor. Her eyes grew wider than the skillet that held her tortillas. Her lips moved, but the words were nowhere to be found. She shook her head and stepped backward.

"No, no, no, no, no…I didn't take that. I don't steal!"

"Well, how'd it get in your purse?" Kim asked.

"I don't know! I don't steal!"

Kim pursed her lips and looked at Melody. "Girl, I'm gon' wait outside. You know what you need to do."

Melody waited until the door closed behind Kim before she spoke.

"Ms. Gloria, how could you?"

"I don't steal! I don't know how that got in my purse. Maybe one of the kids did it."

"My girls were at school, and my nephews don't go in my bedroom, so they wouldn't know about the watch."

"That man. He must've did it."

"What man?"

"Mr. Rob's papa."

"Why would he put this watch in your purse?"

"He's evil." Gloria patted her chest. "I feel it in my spirit."

"You met Enis one time and that couldn't have been for more than a few minutes because he left to go get his Red Cross assistance." Melody put her watch inside of her purse. "I'm so disappointed in you that I don't know what to do. What else have you stolen from my house?"

Once again, Gloria tried to talk but her words wouldn't cooperate. All she could produce in response to Melody's query were tears that streamed down her cheeks.

"I'm going to tell Rob about this and see how he wants to handle it. Please don't come back to my house until we contact you."

Melody held out her palm and wiggled her fingers. Gloria knew what she was asking for. She grabbed her keys from the table near the door, removed the Sumina's house key from the ring, and handed it to Melody. As she released her

ANIMUS

grip of the key, she looked at Melody and muttered, "I don't steal."

19

Melody appeared stone-faced when she got in the car. She gripped the steering wheel at the ten and two positions and stared out the window.

Kim grabbed the Rolex and marveled at the detail. She'd never held one before; hadn't even been within six feet of such an expensive timepiece. She placed the watch in Melody's purse and watched her sister for a few seconds. An opinion and wise crack danced on her tongue, but her instincts told her it wasn't a good time to be an instigator. She could tell from Melody's blank expression that the gravity of being violated by a person she trusted and had given carte blanche access to her home, was sinking in.

"I'm sorry this happened, Sis." Kim placed her hand on top of Melody's right hand. "You want me to drive?"

Melody shook her head. After a few blinks of her eyes her trance was broken. She started the car and uttered

ANIMUS

robotically, "I can't believe she stole from us. She's never done that before."

"You mean, you've never *caught* her doing that before. Girl, your house is so big that she might've been robbing y'all blind and y'all didn't even notice it. Hell, y'all had two bikes, that must've cost three hundred dollars each, in your shed and you forgot you had 'em."

"Yeah, but what was she going to do with this watch? She couldn't walk around with it on her wrist. A blind person could see she can't afford it."

"What you think she was gon' do with it? She was gon' sell it. Probably take it to some pawn shop around here."

"The watch is registered and insured. She can't just take a Rolex to a pawn shop. The moment I noticed it missing, I'd call the police and then file an insurance claim. The first thing the police would do is contact the local pawn shops. I don't think Gloria is stupid enough to expose herself that way."

"Then she was probably gon' sell it on the streets for pennies on the dollar."

"We pay her well. She's living in our house rent free. We bought her a car. That old woman ain't wanting for nothing."

"Maybe she's a gambler."

Melody allowed that comment to take a few laps around her mind for a moment.

"Now that I think about it, she does go to the casino once or twice a month."

"Mel, y'all see that old woman two times a week. Ain't no tellin' what she's doing or where she's going those other five days of the week. Have you been to the casino?"

"A couple of times. Not often."

"Girl, you know that one of my jobs in New Orleans is at Harrah's Casino. Baaaaby, during the weekday—when the rest of the world is at work—that damn casino be filled with senior citizens. They be in there with walking canes, electric wheelchairs, oxygen tanks...child, they be serious about spending that retirement and Social Security check. And they don't just stay for an hour. They be in there for six and seven hours straight. I'll bet Gloria be in that WinStar Casino in Oklahoma, gambling her ass off."

"I don't know. You're probably right." Melody said as she turned on Virginia Parkway. "I got my watch back, now I've got to go deal with this family feud at my house."

"Sis, sometimes those wounds run deep. And I've gotta keep it real wit'cha, there is something about him."

"Who?"

"Enis. I can't put my finger on it. Like I said, he comes across as nice, but he has weirdo eyes."

Melody thought about the way Enis looked at her when she brought those clothes to his bedroom door.

"On top of that," Kim continued, "if he did half the stuff that Robert says he did, I'd probably have a hard time getting past my issues with him too. Honestly, I wouldn't trust him...not just yet. I definitely wouldn't leave Faith and Hope alone with him."

"Don't worry about that. We've already had that talk with him. If he is caught alone with the girls, he's out of there. Besides, he won't have a chance to be alone with the girls with you and the boys there."

"Yeah, about that. I've got my Red Cross and FEMA vouchers now."

"And?" Melody asked in her big sister tone.

"And...I'm going to look for an apartment in a few days."

"But I thought you were going to stay with us."

"Girl, you know I love and appreciate y'all, but I can't stay at your house much longer. Especially, since creepy Enis is there." Kim noticed the disappointment on Melody's face. "Look at it this way, getting an apartment is the first step toward laying down roots here, right?"

"I guess you're right." Melody smiled and swung a left into her subdivision. "Hell, I might need some place to come and hang out if Robert and Enis don't learn to get along."

"It might be too late for that, Sis." Kim pointed. "Is that a police car and ambulance in front of your house?"

"Oh shit," Melody said and pulled alongside the curb two houses away from hers, "something has happened."

"And it doesn't look good," Kim agreed.

As Melody and Kim raced toward the house, two paramedics pushed a gurney out of the front door. The body atop the gurney was strapped on but appeared to be trying to move—that was a good sign. The boys were outside. Johnny knelt on one knee. Josh sat on the basketball. Jalen stood with his arms crossed.

"Jalen, what's going on?" Kim shouted.

The boys all turned around. Josh ran to his mother and hugged her.

"Uncle Rob beat up his daddy," Jalen said.

"He beat him up bad too," Johnny added.

"Why?" Kim asked.

"I don't know. When we came from the park the police were already here. They wouldn't let us go inside."

"Where's Hope and Faith?" Melody asked.

"Inside talking to the police. I heard the policeman say Faith called 9-1-1."

Melody and Kim stormed through the front door like a pair of DEA agents.

"Ma'am, you can't be in here," a petite white female officer said and held up her arms.

"This is my house, I can be wherever the hell I want," Melody replied and hit the officer with a swim-move that would have made an NFL coach proud. Kim was on her sister's heels. "Where are my daughters!"

"They're over here, ma'am," said a bald head, muscular, black officer. "They're fine. Two brave little girls you have here."

ANIMUS

Faith and Hope both bear-hugged Melody.

"I'm their aunt," Kim said. "What happened?"

"Apparently, their father beat up their grandfather."

"Why?" Melody asked.

"No one knows, ma'am. Your daughters saw the two men fighting, and since you weren't here, the one named, Faith called 9-1-1. Which was the right thing to do," the officer added.

"Where is my husband?"

"We have him in custody, ma'am. He's being arrested for assault. Your father-in-law is being taken to Medical City of McKinney to have his bruises treated and for further assessment." The officer dug into his breast pocket and pulled out two business cards. He gave one to Melody and the other to Kim. "You can call the number on that card to track the situation and get instructions on how to proceed."

The officer left the women and two crying girls standing there. Kim wrapped her arms around Melody. By the time the ambulance and police car drove away, the boys were inside the house and had wrapped their arms around their mother and aunt. They were one big fleshly ball of comfort that reflected an all-too common scene whenever domestic violence makes an appearance.

20

"He did what!" EJ propped up on one elbow and jammed his cellphone in the crook of his neck while he groped the darkness in search of the lamp. "Mel, I need you to slow down and say that again."

"What's wrong?" Darlene moaned, struggling to stay tethered to the dream she was enjoying.

"Mel said Rob beat up my dad. She just came back from the police station. She said my dad is at the hospital."

"What time is it?" Darlene asked.

"It's 8:05."

"When did this happen?"

"Mel, when did this happen?" EJ's eyes widened when Mel answered. "That long ago and you're just callin' me?" EJ scrolled through his phone. "Oh, I see I missed your calls. We fell asleep early."

"Is your dad okay?" Darlene asked.

ANIMUS

"She said he has a busted lip, his nose was bleeding, and he hurt his neck," EJ answered. He addressed Melody again. "Alright. I'll head to the hospital and give you an update after I see him."

EJ hung up the phone and put back on the clothes he'd practically ripped off two hours earlier when he and Darlene's most recent argument led to a round of passionate sex. Darlene remained naked under the bedsheets determined to get back to her dream.

"I told you whatever little scheme you and your daddy are up to ain't gon' work. Rob gon' kick yo' ass next."

"I told you there ain't no scheme. Now shut up and go back to sleep!"

"Whatever. Turn off the light and make sure you lock the front door."

It was 8:45 p.m. when the E.R. physician allowed EJ to go into Enis' room. He expected to see his father sleeping, but Enis was reading a magazine with eyes that were so swollen they appeared closed. A lump the size of a golf ball protruded from his forehead. The neck brace Enis wore hindered his ability to turn his head, but he spotted EJ out the corner of his eye.

"Hey, son."

"What's up, Da," EJ said when he entered.

"I was wondering if you were gon' come."

"I came as soon as Mel called and told me what happened." EJ pulled a chair over to the bed and sat down. "How you feelin'?"

"Better than I look."

"What happened to set Rob off?"

Enic chuckled. "You know it don't take much to set your brother off. The boy got anger issues. You know that better than anybody."

"Did y'all get into an argument or something?"

ANIMUS

Enis tossed the magazine on the bed. "We were talking in his office. I went in there to talk to him about our history. I wanted to apologize for anything I've done to upset him."

"C'mon, Da, we both know it's gon' take more than an apology for Rob to get past his issue with you."

"It shouldn't."

"What do you mean it shouldn't? He blames you for mama's death."

"Your mama and I wasn't even together when she committed suicide."

"Well—"

"Well, nothing," Enis snapped and adjusted his posture in the bed. "I didn't make her take those pills."

EJ staired aimlessly at the floor and started recounting the day his mother died.

"I was having a good day the day it happened. Domonique, the prettiest girl in school, gave me her phone number after I stopped a bully from harassing her." Enis smiled slightly. "Domonique and I were going to our sixth period class when assistant principal pulled me to the side and told me to come to her office. When I walked in her office and saw Rob and Uncle Lionel, I knew something bad had happened." EJ pursed his lips and shook his head as the images crept back to the forefront of his mind. "Honestly, my first thought was that you'd died. Don't ask me why, but when I saw your brother with Rob, that's what I thought. They wouldn't tell me what was going on until we got in the car. I remember sitting in the backseat and looking at them getting more and more pissed. The more I asked what was going on, the more they ignored me.

"Uncle Lionel drove to the Lakefront and parked. He told me to get out of the car so we could talk. Rob just buried his head between his legs and started crying…hard. That's when Uncle Lionel told me that mama swallowed a bottle of sleeping pills." EJ used his middle finger to wipe the tear forming in the corner of his eye. "I couldn't believe it. I was shocked. I walked up on that hill on the Lakefront and sat there for about thirty minutes. Rob had to come get me."

"I didn't make yo' mama take those pills. I didn't buy 'em and I didn't put 'em in her hand. I'm sorry that happened, but yo' mama made the decision to take her life. Hell, I was hurt by it too. Your mama is the only woman I've ever loved." Enis sighed. "I'm gon' ask you a straight question and I want you to give me a yes or no answer. Did you ever see me put my hands on your mama?"

EJ thought for a moment. He dug deeper into the corridors of his mind than ever before but came up empty. "No."

"Thank you," Enis said triumphantly and grabbed the magazine. He flipped to the article he was reading when EJ arrived. "Your brother got problems that ain't got nothin' to do with me."

A nurse rapped on the door and then entered the room.

"I'm sorry, sir, but I'm going to have to ask you to leave. It's nine o'clock. Visiting hours are over."

"How long you gon' be in here?" EJ asked.

"The doctor said they're keepin' me tonight for observation, but I should be getting out tomorrow afternoon."

EJ patted Enis' covered leg. "Call me when you check out, and I'll come get you."

"EJ...are you still with me?"

"What?"

"I said...are you *still* with me?"

"Yeah," EJ said half-heartedly. "Sometimes I wonder why, but yeah...I'm still with you."

Melody spent the rest of the night in Hope and Faith's bedroom trying to console them. She welcomed their desire to cuddle and rest their heads on her shoulders. The trauma of

ANIMUS

seeing their father hauled off in handcuffs and their grandfather carted away on a gurney left them shaken to their core. Melody assured them that everything would work out and their father would come home soon; but even she wasn't sure what the outcome would be.

It was 10:30 when their questions stopped, and their eyelids slammed shut. Melody stared at the ceiling trying to figure out what to do next.

The call from Robert came a few minutes before 11:00 p.m. Melody slid out of bed, careful not to wake the twins, and whispered, "Hello."

"Hey, baby, it's me."

"Rob, where are you now?"

"I'm still at the jail. They let me make a phone call. How are the girls doing?"

"How do you think they're doing? They are upset...and so am I. What the hell happened?"

"It's a long story. He said some shit that set me off. It's too much to get into now. Where is he?"

"You damn near beat him to death. Where do you think he is? He's at the hospital."

"Damn."

"Damn is right, Robert. What am I supposed to do?"

"I want you to call, Morris Collier, the district attorney. My company has been doing the landscaping at his house for years. His phone number is in that organizer on my desk. Explain to him that I got into it with my dad, but no one died or anything like that. I need him to make some calls, so they'll release me. Once I'm out, I'll get an attorney and move forward from there."

"Alright. Are you doing okay?"

"Yeah, I'm in a holding cell by myself. You know what, don't call the D.A. tonight...it's too late. Call him first thing in the morning."

"Okay."

"Baby, I'm sorry. I just—"

ANIMUS

"Let's talk about it tomorrow, Rob. I'm stressed out and tired."

"Alright. Well, kiss the girls for me. Let 'em know I love them, and I should be home tomorrow. I love you too."

"I love you too," Melody said. "And I've got something to tell you too. It's about Ms. Gloria."

"Did something happen to her? Is she okay?"

"Yes, something happened. And yes, she's okay. But we'll talk about it tomorrow."

21

September 6, 2005/McKinney, TX.
8:33 a.m.

Since the night before had produced more fireworks than a 4th of July celebration, Melody thought it best to let the twins stay home from school. She didn't even bother to wake them, figuring it was best to allow them to get as much physical and mental rest as their young bodies needed.

Kim prepared a pot of coffee for her and Melody. They sipped slowly and said little while sitting at the island. They both flinched when the doorbell rang.

"I'll get it," Kim said.

She took another sip of her coffee and answered the door.

ANIMUS

"Hey, EJ."

"What's up Kim." EJ's dejected tone and the worry etched on his face told the story of his night. "Is Mel up?"

It was the first time in all the years they'd known each other that he hadn't made a pass at her. That was a clear indicator to Kim of how serious things were.

"Come on in. Mel's in the kitchen."

The scent of chicory coffee invaded EJ's nostrils before he made it to the kitchen. "You got some more of that?"

"Have a seat," Kim said. "I'll pour you a cup."

"Thanks. Give it to me black. What's up, Sis?"

"Hey," Melody replied dejectedly.

EJ and Melody hugged.

"You alright?" EJ asked.

"About as well as can be expected. It's the girls I'm worried about. They are traumatized by what they saw."

"I'll bet." EJ took the coffee cup from Kim. "Thanks."

"How's your dad?" Melody asked.

"He's good. I was able to see him for a few minutes last night before they kicked me out of the hospital. He's a little bruised up, but he'll survive. How is Rob?"

"He's okay. He called me late last night. I just got off the phone with the D.A. He's going to get Rob released this morning. But he said Rob can't come back here until this mess gets hashed out. He said he might have to bring simple assault charges against Rob. Not that he wants to, but he has to follow the law. I asked him if there was any way to get the charges dropped, and he said your dad would have to convince him that this was just a misunderstanding."

"What happened?" Kim asked.

EJ took a sip of his coffee and placed the cup on the counter. He stared at the cup as if the answer to Kim's question would appear in the liquid.

"My dad said he went to talk to Rob. Said he wanted to apologize to Rob about the things in their past. He said Rob just lost it and started swinging on him."

ANIMUS

"I know my husband; he wouldn't have gone crazy like that unless something was said."

"I know Rob too," EJ said. "I've known him longer than you. He's always had a temper."

"That may be true, but he has a lot of self-control. Something was said that triggered him. We both know about y'all past and all the stuff that happened."

EJ took another drink and said, "Actually, we don't."

"What do you mean?" Melody asked and shot EJ a sharp look.

"I mean…Rob has some issues with my dad about stuff that supposedly went on in the past, but—"

"Supposedly. What do you mean, *supposedly*? You tryin' to say Rob made up all the stuff that he said happened between your mom and dad? You're callin' Rob a liar?"

"All I'm sayin' is that I don't remember the stuff Rob said happened. I don't have the same resentment toward my dad that Rob has. We have two different perspectives on our childhood."

"You never saw your dad beat your mama?" Kim asked.

"No, I didn't. I remember some yellin'. I even remember seeing him punch a wall. But I can honestly say to both of y'all that I don't ever remember seeing my dad beat up my mama."

"So, you never knew why she left him?" Melody asked.

"Mel, how many families you know in the 'hood that have mamas and daddies together?"

"That's true," Kim said.

Melody cut her eyes at her sister.

Kim threw up her hands. "I'm just sayin', it's the truth. We grew up in an environment where the two-parent home was a myth. Most of my girlfriends when I was growing up lived with their mamas and saw their daddies on the weekend—if they saw them at all."

ANIMUS

"Exactly," EJ said. "I just figured our parents split up like everybody else's parents. The shit was normal. We didn't ask questions. You just went with the flow."

"You ain't never see your daddy beat your mama?" Melody asked again.

"Mel, you can ask me that same question a million times and my answer gon' still be *no*. Rob has told me stuff about my dad beating my mama. Every story Rob tells me happened when he was under the age of ten. Rob is five, almost five and a half, years older than me. If the domestic violence he's talking about happened up until Rob was ten, that means I was barely five years old." His eyes toggled between Melody and Kim. "I challenge either of you to tell me a story about *anything* that happened to y'all before the age of five."

The sisters both looked off into the distance as they tried to recall a story that would shoot down EJ's theory.

"My point exactly! Y'all can't remember nothin' because our memories don't go that far back. My brother wants me to hate my daddy for some shit, I don't recall happenin'. I can't do that, Mel. I'm not sayin' my Pops was perfect. I'm just sayin' he ain't never do nothin' to me to make me hate him. And I didn't see him do anything to our mama to make me hate him. So, why should I hate him?"

EJ finished off his coffee with an extended gulp and then slid off the bar stool. "Look, I'm gon' get my Pops from the hospital today. Since the D.A. told Rob to not come back here until all of this gets straightened out, is it okay if I bring him back over here?"

"I guess so," Melody mumbled. "But you've got to talk to your dad and ask him not to press charges against Rob."

"I ain't worried 'bout that. My Pops ain't tryin' to put his own son in jail."

"Yall need to put y'all heads together and try to get those two in a room together and settle their differences," Kim said. "I'm talkin' about an intervention like they do on that television show."

Animus

"I think you're right," EJ said. He gave Melody a hug. "Don't worry, Sis, we gon' get this figured out. My Pops gon' be out of here before you know it and y'all can go back to living your lives."

Kim walked EJ to the door and locked it behind him. When she returned to the kitchen, she came armed with questions.

"Umm, I know this isn't any of my business, but I've got to know."

"Know what?"

"What's the story behind Robert's mother? I mean it's clear that Robert and his daddy don't get along. And I know you told me that his mama died when he was younger. But I don't remember you ever telling me how she died."

"Robert doesn't like to talk about it."

Kim looked around the room to drive home the point that they were alone.

"Sis, Rob ain't here."

"Damn you are nosy."

"What's new?" Kim snapped her fingers. "C'mon, give up the details."

Melody did a quick scan to make sure the twins weren't lurking.

"You already know that Enis was physically abusive to Ms. Crystal, Robert's mama."

"Yes, I've heard about that."

"Supposedly, Enis threatened to kill Ms. Crystal. He told her that if he couldn't have her no one else would. She told Robert because she was terrified."

"I would've been too."

"Robert came home the next day and found his mother in the bathroom. He knocked on the door several times, but she wouldn't answer or come out. He got nervous and kicked the door open."

"Oh no," Kim moaned.

ANIMUS

Melody nodded. "Found her on the floor with an empty pill bottle next to her."

"All because she feared Enis."

"Yeah, I guess so."

"Girl, that's so sad. I can't imagine living in that much fear."

"A lot of women do."

"Well, I wouldn't. I would've packed my kids up and left."

"That is so easy to say, Kim, but until you find yourself in that situation, you never know what you'll do. Ms. Crystal was legitimately scared of him. You got some crazy men out there and you never know how far they'll go to hurt you. That's why some women are afraid to fight back; it's easier to just live with the abuser. They go along to get along."

"I see why Robert hates him. I'd hate his ass too." Kim stared at her coffee cup and then segued into something that she'd been pondering. "No disrespect, Sis, but you got a lot of negative energy floating around here, and I don't want my boys exposed to it. I know I said I was going to wait a few days to start looking for an apartment, but I'm gon' start tomorrow."

"Is it because of what I just told you? Kim, that was over twenty years ago. Enis has changed. Besides, he's no threat to you."

"I hear you," Kim said and hugged herself, "but he gives me the creeps. I told you he has weirdo eyes. He shot me a creepy look even when he was tellin' us about Gloria stealing your watch. And that story you just told me doesn't help. I just think it's time for me and the boys to get our own place."

Melody started to protest but decided not to. Kim moving into an apartment in the McKinney area was better than her leaving and trying to go back to New Orleans. At least it all but guaranteed that she'd been in Texas for a year—the length of her lease.

"Alright, I won't fight you. But you know you don't have to leave."

ANIMUS

"I know."

"Well, you can drive my old Lexus. I haven't touched it since Rob bought me the Audi. The Lexus needs a tune up and an oil change, but other than that, it drives fine. I'll tell Robert to get it serviced."

"Thanks, Sis."

"Since you're leaving me, I guess I need to spend as much time as I can with you."

"Stop being dramatic. I'm gon' be right here in the same city."

"Whatever. Let's go grab something to eat. I want to take you to a place I like called, Mi Cocina."

"Sounds Mexican."

"You're in Texas now, and you gon' eat some Mexican food whether you want to or not."

Kim crossed her arms. "Whatever. I ain't gon' like it."

"You gon' still eat it."

"You ain't the boss of me."

"I may not be the boss of you, but I'm the oldest."

"And?"

"And I'm gon' sponsor another shopping spree, so you gon' do what I say."

Kim and Melody locked eyes. Neither blinked. The only thing missing from the moment was western music in the background signaling an impending battle.

"Alright," Kim said and smiled. "But I'm telling you now, I'm not gonna like it."

Melody smirked. "I thought you'd see it my way."

22

EJ pulled his car up to the front entrance of the hospital. Less than three minutes later, the doors opened and Enis came out in a wheelchair being pushed by a beautiful nurse. The neck brace he wore prevented him from craning his neck to look back at the woman, but EJ could tell by the way she blushed that whatever his father said was not meant to be heard by kids under eighteen.

Enis got out of the chair and into EJ's car.

"A wheelchair. Really?"

"Hospital policy," Enis said. "Look at her. When was the last time you seen a white girl with an ass like that?"

"What did you say to her when y'all came out? She damn near turned red in the face."

"I asked her if she liked black men."

"Da, you can't say stuff like that, bruh."

"I can say what the hell I want."

EJ drove off without responding.

ANIMUS

"I can't wait to get back to my bed."

"Da, you talk like you plan on stayin' at Rob's crib forever."

"Maybe. Maybe not."

"As soon as Rob gets out of jail, he's gonna kick you out of his house."

"We'll see."

"You act like you got leverage."

"Son, I've got more leverage than you think." Enis pointed at his neck brace. "I figure it's time me and my oldest son have a little chat..." Enis looked out the window and mumbled. "...about a lot of things."

When they pulled into Rob's driveway, Melody opened the front door. She stood there like she was waiting for the mailman. In some ways, EJ was the mailman. He was delivering a human package that had to remain there because it had no return to sender address.

EJ noticed that Enis' limp became more pronounced when he got out of the car. His posture was more hunched, and he winced a lot more than he had during their drive from the hospital.

"Hey," Melody said. "How are you feeling?"

"I'll make it," Enis replied sounding like he was ready to be placed on life support. He looked at EJ and winked. "I just need to lay these old bones down. Where are my babies? I know they were upset by what they saw. I just wanna let 'em know I'm okay."

"Yes, they were upset," Melody said as she grabbed Enis' elbow, "but they'll be okay. They are strong little girls."

Melody waved at EJ as they went inside to let him know it was okay for him to leave. EJ waved, looked at his laboring father and mumbled, "And the Oscar goes to."

ANIMUS

The activity over the previous twenty-four hours left EJ tired and yearning to get a few hours of shut eye when he made it home. He parked and hopped out of his car before the horses under his hood could stop roaring. He opened the door and started unbuttoning his shirt but was stopped in his tracks by Hurricane Darlene.

"Who the fuck you been callin'?" Darlene shouted.

"What?"

"Nigga is ya' deaf? Darlene waved a sheet of paper. "Whoooo the fuuuuck you been callin' four and five times a week for the past two weeks? I got the phone bill right here."

Darlene shoved the paper in his chest and stood in front of him. While EJ studied the bill, she unzipped his pants and shoved her hand inside.

"Dammit, Dee, what you doin'?"

"Stop askin' that dumb ass question every time I unzip your pants. You know what the hell I'm doing. It's ball check time."

She fondled his balls and dick and then pulled her hand out and smelled it.

"Un-huh, you don't smell nothin' because I ain't done nothin'."

EJ balled up the paper and tossed it in her face.

"Just because you don't have pussy-dick don't mean you ain't been doin' nothin." Darlene picked the paper up and grabbed his arm. "You still ain't explained whose phone number this is." She held the paper up inches in front of his face. "The number circled in red. Whose number is this, EJ?"

"Girl, leave me alone. Call the damn number if you wanna know whose number it is."

"Trust me, I started to call it, but I decided not to. All the bitch was gon' do is play dumb and then hang up and call you to give you a heads up. Nawh, it ain't goin' down like that. I decided to wait until I had yo' ass right here in front of me, so we can call the number together." She wiggled her fingers in front of him. "Give me your phone."

ANIMUS

"Dee, I'm tired. Leave me alone so I can go to sleep."

"Oh, you think I'm playin'." She marched into the kitchen and returned holding the same butcher's knife she'd threatened him with after he shoved her against the wall a few days earlier. "I ain't playin', EJ! Give me your phone so we can call this heifer right now."

EJ looked at the knife and then at Darlene's twitching eyes. He could blow off her demand, but wasn't confident that if he went to sleep, he'd have a dick when he woke up. He pulled out his cell phone and offered it to her.

"No, you call the number. And put it on speaker phone so I can hear the conversation."

EJ dialed the number.

"Look at 'cha, you don't even have to look at the paper. You know it by heart."

The phone rang a few times and then a woman answered.

"Karen Gaston."

"Oh my God, this nigga is cheatin' on me with a white bitch!" Darlene raised her hands like she was reaching for the heavens and paced in a circle for a few rotations before she stopped and put the knife next to EJ's throat. Through pressed lips, she mumbled, "Talk to her, nigga. Act like I ain't here."

"Uh, yeah, Karen," EJ stuttered, "this is EJ."

"Oh, hey EJ. It's good to hear from you I was just going to call you."

Darlene pulled her hands close to her body and gestured like Florida Evans from Good Times when she found out James died.

"Yeah, what's up?" EJ asked.

"I was going to call to tell you somethin' I know you wanna hear."

Darlene lost it. She snatched the phone out of EJ's hand. "What you think he wanna hear? Huh! Huh! What you got to tell my man, Ka-reeeen?"

"Excuse me. Who is this?"

ANIMUS

"This is the woman that's gon' break a foot off in yo' ass, Ka-reeeen! I wanna hear what you gotta tell my man. Matter of fact, I wanna know what you been tellin' my man for the past two weeks."

"Oh, Mrs. Sumina."

"That's right, Ka-reeeen. This is Mrs. Darlene Suuminnna! Now you better start talkin' or else I'm gon' kill him and then I'm comin' to find you."

"Umm, mu, mu, ma'am."

"Muma, muma, my ass. Speak up, tramp!"

"Ma'am, I'm a realtor. I've been working with your husband to find you guys a new home. That's why we've been talking a lot over the last two weeks. I was going to call EJ to tell him I've found the perfect house for you guys. One that you qualify for and has everything in it that he requested. He didn't tell you because he wanted it to be a surprise."

Darlene looked like she'd shitted in her pants. She appeared to be moving in slow motion when she gave the phone back to EJ. It took everything in EJ's power to keep from laughing.

"Karen, I'm sorry about the misunderstanding. I'll call you later so that we can discuss the house. My wife and I need to have a little discussion."

"I understand," Karen said, sounding shook up. "I hope I didn't cause any problems."

"You didn't," EJ assured her. "I'll call you back."

EJ hung up, shoved the phone back into his pocket, and stared at Darlene. Darlene just stood there with her mouth partially open.

"You feel stupid, don't you?"

Darlene nodded.

"You still gon' stab me with that knife?"

Darlene shook her head and dropped the knife on the floor.

"What you got to say for yourself?"

ANIMUS

Darlene's body started to quake, and then, without warning, she erupted. "Ahh!" Darlene jumped into EJ's arms. "Thank you! Thank you! Thank you, baby!"

"Crazy ass," EJ mumbled and carried her into the bedroom.

Robert came out of the jailhouse tucking his shirt into his pants and moving swiftly; like he'd stolen something and was afraid of being collared by the guard at the door. Melody sat in her car with the engine running. She wore dark shades and a baseball cap, looking every bit like an antsy getaway driver.

"Step on it, sweetie. I don't wanna ever see this place again. I just need to get home and take a hot shower."

"You can't."

"What?"

"One of the things the District Attorney stressed when I spoke to him is that you can't stay in the house—not while your dad is there."

"Wait a minute, that's my house!"

"No, that's *our* house. And I can't be having you and your dad fighting in front of my children."

"You sayin' you agree with the D.A.?"

"I'm saying our daughters are traumatized by what they saw their daddy do. I'm saying that I don't want them to ever see that side of you. I'm saying that if your dad—who is at the house right now—brings out that kind of ugliness in you, I don't want you around him. If that means you have to go stay in a hotel for a week until he leaves, then so be it."

"Why can't he go to the hotel? It's my house."

"First you beat your father up and then you wanna put him out. How do you think that's going to look in the eyes of the judge if—or when—you have to go to court?"

"Not good," Robert mumbled.

"It's going to make you look like a bully."

171

ANIMUS

Robert rubbed his unshaven face and smacked the dashboard in frustration.

"Robert! What the hell is wrong with you? You're acting like a lunatic. Calm the fuck down!"

Robert's face contorted like he'd just bitten into a grapefruit. He could count on one hand the number of times he'd heard Melody curse. And none of those, less than handful, of times was the curse word directed at him. Initially, he was taken aback, but he quickly realized that her reaction was in response to his volatile behavior and justified.

"I'm sorry. This situation with my dad has got me pinging off the walls. I don't want you or the girls to view me as some type of loose cannon."

"What happened? EJ told me—"

"How could EJ tell you anything? He wasn't there."

"No, he wasn't, but he went and visited your dad last night in the Emergency Room. Enis told him that he was just trying to talk to you, and you went off. Is that true?"

"I went off because he said some slick shit about my mother."

"Was it slick enough to justify you beating him up in front of your kids?"

Robert didn't answer.

"Do you realize how hypocritical you look right now? On one hand, you tell 'em to never let a man hit 'em because domestic violence is wrong. On the other hand, you are committing domestic violence in front of them by beating up a man that's over sixty years old. Do you know what Faith asked me last night?"

"What?"

"She asked me if you were going to beat her because she called the police."

"C'mon Mel, you know I would never lift a finger to you or my girls."

"I used to know that."

ANIMUS

Robert attempted to touch Melody's hand, which was on the gear shift, but she moved it.

"Now I can't even touch your hand." Robert shook his head frustratingly and looked out the window. "Last night you said something about Ms. Gloria. What happened to her?"

Ms. Gloria's face and the Rolex watch flashed in Melody's mind. Her anger spiked.

"She stole from us."

"What!"

"You heard me…she stole from us."

"What did she steal?"

"My Rolex."

"What! I don't believe that. That woman wouldn't—"

"I got it back from her myself, Robert. Kim and I went to her house and confronted her. The watch was in her purse."

Robert's mouth hung open as he stared out the front window. "I can't believe it."

"I didn't believe it either when your dad told me."

"When my dad told you. What did he tell you?"

"He told me he thought he saw Ms. Gloria coming out of our bedroom wearing a shiny, expensive-looking watch. I went and checked the jewelry box that I keep on the dresser, and sure enough, my Rolex was missing. That's why Kim and I left yesterday evening." She looked at Robert. "You know, when you went *Mike Tyson* on your dad."

"I deserve that." Robert looked out his window again. "I still can't believe she did that. I have to practically beg her to take my money. She's never stolen anything from us before."

"That we know of."

"That we know of," Robert repeated begrudgingly. "I need to talk to her."

"You can talk to her all you want. I don't want her back at the house."

"But baby—"

ANIMUS

"I mean it Rob! I can deal with a lot, but I can't stand a thief."

Robert sighed and leaned his head back on the headrest. "So, how do you wanna play this?"

"You look a mess." Melody looked at the blood stains on Robert's shirt and then eyed his grizzled chin. His body odor was also noticeable. "I allowed the girls to stay home from school today because they were upset, but I don't think it's a good idea for them to see you looking like this."

"I agree."

"You'll have more than enough time to talk to them, but for now, I think you should grab some clothes and go get a room." She turned onto their block. "I'll go inside and pack you a duffle bag with some underwear and clothes. You sit in the car. When I bring the bag out, you can take your car and go get a room. Just call me and let me know which hotel you're staying in."

"Okay."

Melody pulled into the driveway. When she grabbed the gear shift to put the car in park, Robert grabbed her hand.

"Love, I'm sorry."

Melody looked at his hand on top of hers. "I know you are." She used her thumb to caress his knuckles. "Enis will be gone in a few days and things will go back to normal."

23

September 7, 2005/McKinney, TX.
1:11 p.m.

After Melody packed a duffle filled with clothes and brought it out to Robert, they kissed—it was more like a peck—and he left. He stopped at a nearby liquor store and grabbed a pint of whiskey and then drove to a nearby Hampton Inn and checked in. With his worries weighing him down like an anvil, Robert took a long hot shower, finished off half the bottle of whiskey and was snoring within an hour.

When Robert's eyes opened, it was the next day. He took advantage of the hotel's Continental breakfast and did something he rarely did—relaxed. While lying in bed watching

ANIMUS

SportsCenter, he grabbed his cellphone and called the office to get an update on all activity. The reports were good, so he ended the calls and called Melody.

"Hello."

"Hey, Love, it's me. Did I wake you?"

"I'm just being lazy. I'm glad you called. I needed to get my butt out of bed. I want to plant some flowers that I bought and then start prepping dinner."

"Where is everyone?"

"The girls went to school today. Kim left with her boys. They are going apartment hunting."

"She's moving out?"

"Yeah, she wants to give us some space to work out our issues. She's driving my car. Which reminds me...I need you to get the Lexus serviced. I told her she can use it."

"I'll take care of it."

"Thanks. She's going to pick up the girls from school for me."

"That's good. Gives you some time to yourself. I know you need it. As far as her looking for an apartment, I can't say that I blame her. It's been crazy around there."

"Yes, it has."

"So, ummm, is Enis there?"

"Yeah. I guess he's in his room sleeping."

"I've been doing a lot of thinking about everything that's happened and some of the things Dr. Miles told me. I'm going to come over this evening and talk to the girls. While I'm there, I'm going to talk to Enis to see if we can straighten things out."

"Are you sure you can handle that?"

"Yeah, I'm sure. I promise you; I won't do anything crazy."

"Are you sure, Rob? Because the children—"

"Love, I promise you...I'm good. I'll be on my best behavior. Now, can I come home?"

Melody sighed. "Yes, you can come home."

"Cool."

"It should be close to checkout?"

"Damn, you're right. Checkout is at eleven. If I hurry, I can make it."

"Don't rush. I think one more day for things to calm down will do us all some good. Just come home in the morning."

"Okay. Babe, I love you."

"I love you too."

Robert hung up and smiled. The hotel room was nice, but it wasn't his home. He'd make the best of it for one more day but planned to be back at his house in time to take his daughters to school the next morning.

There is still something I need to do, Robert thought.

He put on a jogging suit and a pair of tennis shoes and headed out.

"Who is it?" Ms. Gloria shouted.

"It's me, Ms. Gloria! Robert!"

It took a few seconds, but Ms. Gloria finally opened the door. "I'm not a thief, Mr. Rob!"

Robert held up his hands to calm her down. "I know you're not a thief, Ms. Gloria. I just came over here to talk to you. I wanna hear your side of the story."

Ms. Gloria backed away from the door to allow him to enter.

"You want something to drink? I have tea and coffee."

"Some tea will be fine."

Robert sat down and waited patiently for Ms. Gloria to return. Moments later, she emerged from the kitchen holding a cold glass of tea and a plate of quesadillas.

"You look hungry. I made quesadillas. You like my quesadillas."

"Thanks Ms. Gloria. And you're right, I am hungry."

ANIMUS

She watched him take a bite. Studying him as if she was waiting for a reaction. Robert knew her all too well. She was no different than any grandmother who seeks validation in her cooking.

"You still make the best quesadillas, Ms. Gloria," he said and smiled while chewing. "Now, tell me what happened."

"Your papa, that's what happened!"

"What do you mean?"

"I run over and over in my head. How did that watch get in my purse?" She pointed at Robert. "I don't steal! You know I never steal from you before!"

"I know you don't steal, Ms. Gloria."

"I saw your papa coming out of your office."

"When?"

"Monday, when I went to clean your house. I told him, only me and Mrs. Mel go in that office. No one else."

"And what did he say?"

"He said he didn't know that. And then later that day, I saw him talking to some men outside."

"What men?"

"I don't know. One big man—looked mean. The other man was short." She held out her hand to show the man's height. "About yea big."

Robert's face scrunched and he scratched his forehead. "Did you hear what they said?"

"I tried. They talk too low. Your papa looked scared. He saw me at the window looking at him talk to the men. When he came inside, I said nothing to him…nothing. I just do my work and leave. Later, Mrs. Mel come and say I took her watch. I don't steal!"

"She said you had the watch in your purse."

"Yes, it was in my purse, but I didn't take it."

Robert sipped his tea and scratched his head again.

"She took her key," Ms. Gloria said. Her eyes filled with water. "I love your family. Mrs. Mel, the girls, you…I would never—"

ANIMUS

"I believe you, Ms. Gloria."

She grabbed the napkin that she brought out with Robert's plate and dabbed her eyes.

"Mr. Rob, can I say something?"

"Sure. What's on your mind?"

"My papa was a brujo in Catemaco."

"What's that?"

"He did the black magic."

Robert leaned back. He wasn't sure where she was going with this, but he could feel the hairs on the back of his neck start to dance.

"When I was a little girl, he used to take me to the top of a hill near our house and talk to me about things."

"What kinds of things?"

"A lot of things. Evil things. He taught me how to spot evil in man." Ms. Gloria crumpled the napkin in her wrinkled hand and leaned forward. "Your papa is evil. I feel it in my spirit. You need to get him out of your house. If you don't, he will infect everything there. Evil must be cut out."

Robert allowed her words to marinate. He knew nothing about brujos or evil spirits, but he did know the importance of listening to his elders. He also knew that what she said about Enis was true. He was evil, and the fact that she was able to surmise that after one encounter added credibility to what she was saying.

She sized his ass up quick. Why was he in my office? Who were those men he was talking to in front of my house? If she had a run-in with him, he probably views her as a threat. Probably was scared she'd tell me what she saw. That means he needed to discredit her. Yeah, that sneaky bastard set her up.

"Ms. Gloria, if I can work this out with Melody will you come back?"

"Not as long as your papa is there. He's evil...very, very, evil. I can feel it in my spirit Mr. Rob."

ANIMUS

"I understand, Ms. Gloria. But if I'm going to get your job back, I have to convince Melody that he's evil. Are you willing to tell Melody everything you told me?"

"Yes."

"Good. Can you come with me now?"

"Yes. I need to put on some clothes."

"That's fine. I'll wait outside in the car."

Thoughts swam around in Robert's head like swimmers at the Olympic tryouts while he sat in the SUV.

Everything is starting to make sense. Enis is running from someone and he used the hurricane as a convenient excuse to come to Dallas and use my house as his hideout. He framed Gloria because she became suspicious. Shit has been fucked up since EJ brought him here. EJ...the common denominator in all of this. EJ knows how I feel about that man, yet he brought him to my home anyway. The two of them are up to something...and I'm going to find out what it is.

Robert started the car. The engine growled. His radio was programmed to go to his favorite radio station, 101 Oldies, and the station did not disappoint.

"This an oldie but goodie by one of the greatest R&B Groups of all time," said the disc jockey with the silky-smooth voice. "This is a classic. *I Love Music* by the O'Jays."

Robert's head bobbed to the harmonies and the smooth voices of the groups lead singers, Eddie Levert and Walter Williams. Suddenly, as if he'd been caught doing something illegal, Robert stopped humming the tune. His fingers stopped strumming the steering wheel. His body became tense. That was his response whenever a song by the O'Jays came on. As much as he loved the group, he hated the memories their songs evoked.

The O'Jays was Enis' favorite group when Robert was a child. In the 1970's, when the group was at it's musical peek and cranking out hit albums yearly, their music was Enis' "mood music" whenever he prepared to go out on the town. Songs like "Living for the Weekend", "She Used to be My

ANIMUS

Girl", "For the Love of Money", and "I Love Music" were in heavy rotation inside the Sumina household on payday Friday.

Enis had a decent singing voice and didn't mind showing it whenever his O'Jays tunes were on the record player and their voices spewed from the speakers of his raggedy "component" set.

As a child of six, seven, and eight years old, Robert had no idea that it was not normal for a married man with two kids to go out to the club on Friday evening and not return until Sunday night. And he didn't know it was not normal for the married man's wife to help her husband get dressed, toss him the keys to the Cutlas Supreme that her father fixed up and gave to her, and then wave cheerfully at her husband as he drove away, knowing she wouldn't see him for two days. He was too young to understand that being stranded in the house because the only vehicle was gone for three straight days wasn't a good thing.

All Robert knew back then was that he and his mother were always the happiest on payday Fridays because those were the only three day stretches when they both knew that neither would be beaten.

"That was one of my favorite jams," said the disc jockey as the song faded. "There's just something about the O'Jays music that puts you in a good mood…don't you agree? Brings back such sweet memories."

The driver side door opened, and Robert flinched.

"I'm ready, Mr. Rob."

Robert turned his head.

"Mr. Rob…are you crying?"

Robert cleared his throat. "No, no…I'm not crying. I had something in my eyes, and I used eye drops to get it out."

Gloria stared at Robert for a moment with that "you're full of shit" look that God reserves for mothers, and then slowly put on her seat belt.

"You sure?" she asked, her eyes staring out the front window.

ANIMUS

"Positive Ms. Gloria," Robert replied and wiped his eyes. He turned off the radio, placed his hand on the gear shift, and put the car in drive. "Let's get going."

Before the car could move, Gloria reached out and gently touched Robert's right hand.

"He's bad," she said and squeezed, "but you're a real good man. Not like him at all."

If words were the cork in a wine bottle, Gloria's words were the cork that kept Robert's emotion trapped. The cork was popped, and a tidal wave of feelings poured out of him.

Gloria never released her grip of Robert's hand. She started to rock in her seat as if she could hear a tune in her head. The more Robert cried, the tune in her head became louder. Eventually it spilled from her mouth. Her pitch was perfect. She sang in Spanish. And although Robert couldn't understand her, he could *feel* her.

Gloria continued to sing, hum, and squeeze Robert's hand. It was what he needed. He didn't have to send out a request for emotional support. She was a mother at heart. She could hear a child's non-verbal cry for help. Even if the child wasn't her own.

24

When Robert and Ms. Gloria arrived at the house, Enis was still in his bedroom. Melody was in the backyard planting flowers.

"Okay, Ms. Gloria, I already called Melody to tell her you are coming to talk to her. She's in the backyard. I want you to go tell her everything you told me. Even the part about seeing my dad outside talking to some mean men."

"Okay." Ms. Gloria affectionately grabbed Robert's arm. "Thank you for believing me. I don't steal."

Robert smiled. "I know you don't."

As Ms. Gloria made her way to the backyard, Robert headed to his office.

If he was in here, he must've been looking for something. I need to see if anything has been moved.

Melody and Kim had put things back in order since the fight. Robert figured nothing was missing, but that didn't stop

ANIMUS

him from making a beeline to his safe. He opened it to see if anything had been removed. Satisfied with his inspection, he moved over to his desk and sat down while he examined the drawers. When he heard the knock on the door, he froze as if he was the one breaking and entering.

"Hey, son," Enis said. "Got a second to talk?"

"Yeah," Robert said. He walked over to a file cabinet and put some papers in it. "I actually came here to talk to you."

"Oh, really?"

Enis sauntered around Robert's office. His hands were behind his back and he moved as if he were in an art gallery studying priceless pieces. He straightened a few crooked picture frames, sprinkled a few flakes of fish food into the fish tank, and then strolled behind the desk and plopped down onto the plush leather seat.

"Now, this is what I'm talkin' about," Enis said. He leaned back in the chair, put his hands behind his head, and planted his feet on the desktop. "I could get used to this."

"You could, but you ain't." Robert stood in the doorway simmering like he was ready for round two. "Are you trying to piss me off?"

Enis smiled and yawned. "I'm just relaxing."

"Unless you want me to beat your ass again, I suggest you get out of my chair."

Enis dismissed his comment with a wave of his hand. "Quit huffing and puffing, son. Close the door and let's have that talk."

"We gon' talk, but first you're going to get out of my chair."

Enis removed his feet from the desktop and leaned forward, making sure his elbows were firmly planted on the desk. "Trust me when I say this, son, you gon' want to close that door. I *know* you don't want Melody to hear what I'm about to say."

Three frown lines created grooves in Robert's forehead deep enough to swim in. He wasn't sure where Enis was going

ANIMUS

with that snide remark, but he knew few words escaped the master manipulator's mouth without him giving them a lot of thought. They were designed to sting, harm, and even maim, if necessary.

Robert closed the door reluctantly. He could feel his blood pressure boiling and no longer wanted to be in Enis' presence.

Enis pointed at the chair adjacent to the desk. "Sit down."

"Talk fast old man and get the hell out of here."

"Fast or slow it don't matter to me. What I have to say will still have the same effect."

"What the hell are you talkin' about?"

"I'm talkin' about your lovechild."

Robert's head tilted in that peculiar way a dog's head tilts when it can't understand its master. He took a step closer. Enis pointed at the chair in front of the desk again. It was the first time Robert had been instructed to sit in the seat he'd put in the office for guests. He sat down slowly, refusing to take his eyes off Enis.

"Yeah, I thought that might get your attention." Enis leaned back in the chair and assumed his same cavalier, hands behind his head, posture. He even punctuated the move by placing his feet back on the desk. "I know your little secret, son. You should probably be nicer to me. Unless you want your wife to know what I know."

"And what is it you *think* you know about me?"

"Ah, ah, ahh…I don't *think* I have some dirt on you, I *know* I have some dirt on you. Matter of fact, it's more than a little dirt. The dirt I have on you qualifies as a sand dune."

"Look man—"

"Don't rush me, son. This is just getting good." Enis examined his fingernails while delivering his death blow. "Remember that night you and your brother went out to party before you had to go back to the base and get ready to ship off to Afghanistan?"

ANIMUS

"What about it?"

"Do you remember what happened that night? No, you probably don't because you were too shit-faced to remember anything. EJ had to practically carry you in the house. You vomited all over the place." Enis smiled. "I know because I had to clean it up."

"Get to your point."

"Okay...since you seem to be in a rush. My point is, EJ told me about your little hook-up with the stripper that night in the bathroom stall."

Robert stared at the floor. He squinted, hoping increased focus would jog his memory. Eventually, it did. The look of anger in his eyes morphed into a look of horror.

"Yeah, you remember the cute little freckled face, long-legged, red bone with the tiny waist and an ass big enough to sit a Coke bottle on it. Her name was Carmen."

Robert nodded as the memory resurfaced. Enis lowered his feet and leaned forward. In a tone that hovered just above a whisper, he went in for the kill.

"You banged sexy Carmen in the bathroom stall, son. I guess you paid for more than a lap dance. Three days later, you were overseas playing soldier in the desert. But what you didn't know is that you left a woman here in the states pregnant."

"EJ told you this?"

"He didn't have to. Ms. Carmen came around looking for you, but you were already gone. I talked her out of pressing you for child support because I knew that Melody would dump you if she knew you cheated on her...especially with a stripper." Enis scratched his chin and looked at his fingernails again. He snapped his fingers and pointed at Robert. "Did I tell you that you have another little girl? Her name is Kayla. I used to have a picture of her, but like everything else, it got washed away in the storm."

"So, you've been in touch with this Carmen chick?"

ANIMUS

"Oh yeah, we kept in touch for at least three years after the baby was born. Kayla is a cutie pie. Not as cute as my girls in there, but she's a cutie pie. Her mama would bring her around to let me see her. I would slip her a few dollars when I could."

"Does EJ know about this?"

Enis shrugged. "Maybe he does, maybe he doesn't. I've never spoke of it. And I don't plan on mentioning anything to anybody…unless…"

"Un-huh, I knew it was coming. That blackmail train ain't never late with you. What…you gon' tell Melody?"

Enis shrugged again. "That depends."

"On what?"

"It depends on how hard of a time you give me about the money I need."

Robert sighed, ran his hand across his face, and put his elbows on his knees. "How much?"

"Twenty thousand."

"When?"

"Today."

"What! Nawh, that ain't gon' happen."

"Robert, you seem to think I'm asking you. Son, I'm tellin' you. Go get my money or I will make sure your pretty little wife in there knows all about Carmen the stripper and baby Kayla."

Robert was trapped between the proverbial rock and a hard place. If he declined Enis' proposition, he had no doubt that Enis would sing like a bird. If he followed the desires of his heart and split Enis' head open to the white meat, Enis would still snitch if he had a slither of life in his body.

Maybe he could deny the affair. But that wouldn't work because he did in fact have the affair. Whether he was drunk at the time it happened was irrelevant, Melody wouldn't care. If she learned of a lovechild, his life would be ruined. Melody would divorce him, take his kids, and half of everything he owned.

ANIMUS

"C'mon, son, study long...study wrong. I taught you to play chess when you were a little boy. I see the chess board over there in the corner, so I know you still play. I got you in check, young king. One more move and it'll be checkmate. Do yourself a favor and just lay down."

Robert's leg fidgeted and his foot tapped the floor. He stared at the floor and shook his head.

"Taking out twenty thousand dollars isn't as simple as you're making it sound. Most banks require a day or two."

"Really? Is that how it works? I wouldn't know nothin' 'bout that. I ain't never took out more than a thousand dollars. Well, just get me 10K for now. You can wire me the rest."

"If I get you this money—"

"*When* you get me this money."

Robert rolled his eyes. "*When* I get you this money, I don't wanna ever see you again."

"You won't...as long as you hold up your end of the bargain." Enis stood up and headed out of the office. "You can have your chair back. I'm going to get something to eat."

"I hate you," Robert mumbled.

"Yeah, I know." Enis grabbed the doorknob and looked back. "But you gon' pay me." He laughed and said, "Checkmate."

Robert made a beeline for the front door. He got in his car and smacked the steering wheel.

"Shit! I can't believe this is happening!"

He backed out of the driveway and called EJ while he made haste toward the bank.

"Yeah," EJ answered.

"EJ, do you remember that night when we went out before I got shipped off to Afghanistan?"

EJ laughed. "Hell yeah! That was the best partying we've ever done."

ANIMUS

"Did I hook up with a stripper named Carmen?"

"You don't remember?"

"Man, I don't remember much of anything from that night."

"Yeah, you hooked up with her. I'm the one who introduced y'all. I went to school with her. She used to mess with a dude I know."

"Shit!"

"Why? What's up?"

"I think I got her pregnant that night."

"What! Nawh bruh, you didn't get her pregnant."

"EJ, you just told me I hooked up with her."

"You did. Matter of fact, you hit in the bathroom stall."

"Damn! Damn! Damn!"

"Calm down, Florida Evans. Yes, you hit it in the bathroom stall. Y'all both were drunk. I smashed her best friend in the next stall. We were all fucked up that night. But you didn't get her pregnant."

"How do you know?"

"Because Carmen couldn't get pregnant."

"How do you know that?"

"I told you I used to fuck her best friend. She had a motor mouth; told me all of Carmen's business whenever they got mad at each other. Carmen had some kind of cyst on her ovaries when she was young. She ended up getting a hysterectomy. That girl couldn't get pregnant if she tried."

"So, she doesn't have a daughter named Kayla?"

"Not that I know of. I know she moved to California and married some dude that has kids. Maybe one of his kids is named, Kayla. Why?"

"That lowdown son-of-a-bitch."

"What's up?"

"Nothing. Thanks, bruh. I owe you. I've gotta go."

"Hey, before you hang up. I need to talk to you about something. Me and Darlene trying to buy a house. I've been

ANIMUS

working with my man Dino—you know the dude that be flipping houses?"

"Yeah."

"Well, for the past year, Dino's been slipping me a few hundred dollars a week to help him renovate houses. I lied and told Dee you've been working me six days a week so she wouldn't figure out I had a side hustle, but on one of my off days with you, I've been working with Dino."

"Yeah, I know about that."

"Well, I didn't tell Dee because I was trying to surprise her and come up with the money to buy the house. She's been wanting me to ask you, but I didn't wanna do that. Anyway, my realtor hit me up. She found a house that's perfect for us, but because of my credit, I've gotta come up with a larger down payment. And umm, I'm a little short."

"How much do you need?"

"About ten grand. I'll pay you back. You can even take it out of my check."

"That's not necessary. I got you."

"What?"

"Nigga did I stutter? I said I got you. Consider this a housewarming gift. I'll get it to you next week."

"Bruh, are you serious?"

"Serious as AIDS. Now, I've gotta go. I'll hit you later."

Robert hung up and yanked the steering wheel. The tires on his SUV squealed as he made a doughnut at the intersection and sped back to his house.

25

When Enis saw Gloria standing outside talking to Melody, he went into his room and pulled out his phone—fumbling it as he dialed. His heart rate quickened from the excitement of knowing he'd finally accomplished his goal.

"Yeah, I got him to agree to give me the money." Enis glanced over when he heard the back door open and close. "I'm whispering because that nosy ass housekeeper is always ear hustling. He's going to get the money now. When he brings it back, I'm getting the hell out of here tonight. I'm gon' keep my end of the bargain. He'll never learn the truth from me. Trust me, my lips are sealed." Enis paused again. "I've gotta go."

Enis hung up the phone and tiptoed over to the bedroom door. He waited a few seconds and then yanked it open. Gloria was on the other side of the door with her ear

ANIMUS

pressed against it. She lurched backward when the door flung open.

"I knew your nosy ass was listening," Enis growled. "How much did you hear?"

"I heard enough to know what's going on. I knew it," Gloria wagged her finger. "I knew you were up to something. I'm going to tell Mr. Rob."

"You ain't gon' do a damn thing," Enis said and grabbed her arm, "because Rob ain't here."

Gloria flashed her teeth like an angry dog flashes its fangs. Enis had no idea what she was about to do, but he felt her intentions when she sunk her teeth into his knuckles.

"You bitch!" Enis released her arm and shook his hand as if that would take away the pain. "I'ma kill you!"

Gloria ran. She headed for the kitchen, but that was as far she could make it. Enis grabbed the back of her collar and shoved her. Gloria fell forward into the countertop. With his left hand still smarting from her bite, Enis used his left hand to deliver a smack that made Gloria spin like a top.

"Ya' see, you flip at the mouth because you ain't never had a man deal with you the right way."

"Help!" Gloria yelled.

Enis clamped his hand over her mouth to silence her, but it was too late. Melody came through the back door, and Robert came through the garage door connected to the hallway that led to the kitchen.

"You stupid bitch," Enis growled. He had his right hand clamped over her mouth and his left arm firmly around her neck. "I'm gon' kill you."

"Enis, let her go!" Melody shouted.

"What the hell is going on in here?" Robert yelled as he entered the kitchen.

Enis didn't turn around. Instead, his evil eyes locked in on his prey. He grunted, but no other words came out of his mouth.

ANIMUS

Robert grabbed Enis by the collar and pulled him backward. Enis fell like a house of cards. His hands were now clasping his stomach—a stomach that spewed blood the way it did in Robert's dream.

"Oh my God!" Melody yelled.

Robert looked at Enis writhing on the floor and then he turned to Gloria. The butcher knife—with its eight-inch blade—quivered in her hand. The blade was lathered in Enis' blood. Her eyes were filled with tears that seemed reluctant to spill. Her trembling made droplets of blood fall from the blade and onto the floor.

"Heeee was…was…going to kill me."

"It's okay," Melody whispered and grabbed Gloria's hand. She had to pry the old woman's fingers from the knife handle to get it out of her possession.

"Mr. Rob…your papa grabbed me and then he hit me." A rogue tear broke free. "He…he…was going to kill me because I heard him." She looked at Melody. "I…I heard him on the phone."

"Robert," Melody said. Robert didn't answer. He was too busy watching his father's blood form a pool around his body. "Robert!" Melody yelled. "We've got to call an ambulance."

Robert shook his head. He inched closer to Enis. The two men made eye contact. Rarely has so many things been said without a word being uttered.

Enis' facial expression softened. The corner of his mouth turned upward. Right before his eyes closed, he mouthed: *I'm sorry.*

"Robert, he's going to die!"

Robert studied the man who'd caused him a lifetime worth of emotional trauma. The man who sent his mother to an early grave. The man whose mere presence brought out the worst in him.

ANIMUS

As if in a trance, Robert moved his foot away from the blood that was slowly making its way toward his shoe. He turned and looked at Melody and said calmly, "Let him die."

26

Uniformed police officers roamed around the Sumina house like ants at a picnic. Paramedics placed Enis' lifeless body inside a bag, zipped it up, and hauled it out of the house on a gurney. A tall balding detective was interviewing Gloria in the living room. A second detective, a plump white man with bad breath and a cowlick that needed to be reworked, interviewed Robert and Melody on the back patio.

"What's going to happen to her?" Melody asked.

"Well, my partner is getting her story now," the detective said and shoved his notepad into the inside breast pocket of a blazer that appeared to be long overdue for a dry cleaning. "I can tell you this…even if it's proven that she killed him in self-defense, she's an illegal alien. I'll bet my pension she's looking at being deported back to Mexico."

Robert appeared more hurt by that comment than the death of his father. Gloria had been his responsibility for years.

ANIMUS

He took care of her financially and treated her like she was his own mother. She returned the affection by treating him like the son she'd lost.

"So, what's next?" Robert asked.

"We're going to take her in. She'll be arraigned in a day or so. That should give you enough time to do whatever you need to do to get her legal representation." The detective shrugged. "That about sums it up. Umm, I'm sorry for your loss, Mr. Sumina."

Robert gave a half-hearted head nod and escorted the detective back inside. Melody sat on the patio sofa and buried her face in the palms of her hands. She remained in that position until the police left their home.

When everyone was gone, Robert stepped back out onto the patio. He sat on the patio chair and draped one leg over the other. His eyes were affixed on the crape myrtle tree he'd recently planted.

"I can't believe this happened," Melody said. "One minute, Gloria was in the backyard helping me plant those flowers; she went inside when I answered my phone and then a few minutes later, I hear her screaming. What do you think happened between those two?"

"She told us what happened. She said she heard him on the phone," Robert peeled his gaze away from the crape myrtle and looked at Melody, "and so did I."

Melody looked quizzically.

"I left the house, but I came right back. When I pulled in the garage, I heard him on the phone."

"How did you hear him on the phone while you were in the garage?"

"I heard him because your Bluetooth was still synced to my car. When he called you and you answered, I heard the entire phone conversation."

Melody swallowed hard. Her eyes bulged. "Baby, let me—"

ANIMUS

"Don't say another word," Robert ordered and held up his hand. "I heard everything. I heard him bragging about getting me to give him the money. I heard him say he was going to leave tonight as soon as he got the money." Robert undraped his leg and leaned forward in his chair. His nostrils flared and the veins in his neck pulsated. He intertwined his fingers and planted his elbows on his knees. "I also heard you beggin' him to not tell me that my girls…are really *his* girls." Robert dropped his head and shook it. "All of this time, I thought he and my brother were up to no good," Robert looked at Melody, "and it was you all the time."

Melody stood up and paced. She placed a hand on her hip and a trembling hand over her mouth while she walked in a tight circle.

"You'd better start explaining…now!"

"He contacted me a few times over the years and asked for a few hundred dollars here and there. I'd send him some money and wouldn't hear from him for months. He contacted me nearly two weeks ago and said he needed ten thousand dollars."

"Why did he want the money?"

"I don't know. He never told me. I assumed it was to pay off a debt or something."

Robert thought about the two mysterious men Gloria saw and mumbled, "Yeah, it was probably a debt." He rubbed his hand over his face in exasperation. "Go ahead, finish."

"I knew there was no way I could get that kind of money without you noticing, so I just told him I'd see what I could do." Melody used the balls of her hands to wipe her tears. "Once the storm hit New Orleans, I didn't think I'd hear from him again. Then, he called me and said he was on his way here. I didn't know what to do."

"So, when EJ brought him here that was all an act?"

"No, it wasn't. I had no idea EJ was going to bring him here. I was just as surprised to see him as you."

ANIMUS

"But when we were in the bedroom, you told me you'd never seen him before. Explain that."

"That was a lie. I first met your dad when I found out you hooked up with that stripper named, Carmen, the night you went out with EJ before you left to go back to your base. I was washing your jeans—because they smelled like vomit—and found her phone number in the pocket. I called her and she said she had sex with you. I was mad at you, Rob! I mean, we weren't married then, but we had a wedding planned for when you returned to the states. I was faithful to you and you were out screwing a stripper in a bathroom stall!"

Robert stared at Melody and didn't utter a word. As far as he was concerned, she was just putting on another award-winning performance at that moment.

"Carmen told me EJ hooked up with her friend that night. So, I went to your dad's house the next day to confront EJ. I wanted to ask him why he'd encouraged you to cheat. But when I got to Enis' house, EJ wasn't home." Melody swiped at her tears again. "Your dad answered the door. When he saw how upset I was, he let me inside and listened to me vent. I had no one else to talk to about the pain I was in…he listened to me. And then," Melody stared out at the crape myrtle and mumbled the rest of her statement, "it just happened."

"Riiight, it just happened. You just *happened* to slip and fall on his dick?"

Melody had no choice but to take the jab. She was already in hot water. Trying to defend her actions would have only made things worse.

"When Enis showed up here, I panicked. That's when I knew he was serious about the ten thousand dollars and would do anything to get it. I was scared he was going to tell you what happened between us, so I agreed to go along with a plan he came up with. I was supposed to talk you into letting him stay here for a while. He was going to use the information about your affair as leverage to pressure you into giving him the money. We figured you'd be so scared he'd tell me about your affair that you'd give him the money and the fact that I slept with him wouldn't have to be mentioned. Once he got the money he would leave and never look back."

"And you believed him?"

"I had no choice. If I didn't cooperate, he was going to—"

"Tell me that *he* is the father of my daughters." Robert banged his fist on the patio table like a judge slamming a gavel. "I can't believe I was so stupid. The truth was right here in my face and I didn't see it. He flaunted the shit in front of my face from the moment he got here." Robert shook his head in disgust. "That sick bastard referred to Faith and Hope as *his babies* the entire time he was here, and I didn't even catch it." Robert smacked the table again. "How could you screw that bastard, Mel? All these years…all these fuckin' years…you let me think those were my girls."

"It was all I could do. You and I made love two nights before you left town. The calendar worked in my favor—less than four days between when we slept together and when I slept with him."

"I can't believe you fucked my dad."

"I was upset when I found out you cheated on me, Rob! But I still loved you and didn't want to lose what we had." Melody untucked her shirt and used the bottom of it to wipe her runny nose. "Enis promised to never say anything. It was our secret…"

"Until he needed some money."

"Yeah," Melody whispered, "until he needed some money."

"I told you he was a hustler," Robert said in a dejected tone. "I told you the man made his living running scams, gambling, and blackmailing people."

"Yes, you did."

The next ten minutes were spent in silence. The Texas sun turned a deep orange and started its descent. Its hairline

ANIMUS

was all that remained as it squatted behind a swath of tall trees in the western skyline.

"What do we do about the girls?" Melody asked. "Should we tell them the truth?"

Robert sighed and stood up. He walked over to Melody and stood close enough to whisper his final remarks into her ear.

"I've raised those girls. I love them more than I love myself. We're not telling *my* daughters that I'm really their brother because their mother fucked their grandfather." Robert paused and shook his head. He wasn't sure if hiding the truth from the girls was the right thing to do, but it was a decision he was prepared to live with. "You wanna make this right?"

"Yes! Baby, I'll do anything to make this right. Just tell me what you want."

The whites of Melody's eyes were pink from the flood of tears. She looked at Robert hoping he'd show mercy.

"Here's what I want from you, Mel. By this time next week, I will be serving you with divorce papers. We will break the news to the girls together. We'll tell them we aren't getting along, and we feel it's best to get divorced. And then I *want* you to pack your shit and get the fuck out of my house. And *our* girls," Robert kissed Melody's forehead, "will be staying here with me…the only man they will ever call, dad."

A Note from the Author

I hope you enjoyed reading my 34th novel, **ANIMUS**. This is my most personal novel since my first novel, *Mama's Lies - Daddy's Pain*. As a result of what I witnessed as a child, I'm fifty-one years old and suffer from PTSD.

My father died when I was eighteen, so the part of the book about him coming to live with me after Hurricane Katrina is not true. The reason why I used Hurricane Katrina as a backdrop for this tale is because it gave me an excuse to address a question that has nagged me for years…what would I do if I could talk to my father today? Honestly, I don't know. But here is what I do know. If you—or someone you know—is in an abusive relationship, you cannot ignore the immediate and long-term psychological effect it has on the children who witness the abuse. You **must** find a way to corral your fear and get out of that relationship. If not for yourself, do it for your kids.

Please tell your friends and family members about the book and take a moment to leave a **BRIEF REVIEW** on Amazon and/or Good Reads. I cannot stress how important your reviews are. By the way, if you do leave a review, **PLEASE DO NOT** give away the surprise ending. Thanks in advance.

Sincerely,
Brian W Smith

Also, by Brian W. Smith

Novels

The S.W.A.P. Game / Mama's Lies – Daddy's Pain / Donna's Dilemma / Nina's Got a Secret / Glass Houses / Larry's Got a Secret Too / BEATER / DIFFERENCES DEADBEAT / If These Trees Could Talk / AMNESIA / HOARDER / QUAGMIRE / THREESOME / BOSS / THREESOME 2 / The Delusion of Inclusion / When the Rabbit's Got the Gun / The Life and Times of Gigolo # 9 / MISSING / Disjointed Custody / Paper Bag

Short Stories

My Husband's Love Child / Close to Home / The Perfect Lie / Lagniappe / Backfire

Sleepy Carter Mysteries

The Audubon Park Murder / A Murder in the Quarters / Passé Blanc / Coffee, Beignets, and Murder

To purchase autographed paperback copies of Brian W. Smith novels, go to his website: www.authorbrianwsmith.com

About the Author

Brian W. Smith is the award-winning, Bestselling Author of thirty-four novels and short stories. His novels have appeared on multiple prominent bestsellers list to include: Dallas Morning News, Amazon, Target, and Black Expressions.

Brian is the Founder/President of *The Script Repository*. The company specializes in adapting novels to screenplays. When Brian is not writing novels, screenplays, and/or ghostwriting novels for others, he serves as an Adjunct Professor of Creative Writing at Collin College (located in suburbs of Dallas, Texas).

Brian was born and raised in New Orleans, Louisiana. He currently resides in Dallas, Texas.

How to contact Brian W. Smith

For book club appearances or speaking engagements, contact the author via email at: bws@authorbrianwsmith.com

To follow the author on social media:

Facebook: www.facebook.com/AuthorBrianWSmith
Instagram: authorbwsmith
Twitter: @AuthorBWSmith